The chi

"Have a seat."

Clint sat down. The chief seated himself behind his desk. "I'd like to thank you for coming in."

"No problem. What's on your mind, Chief?"

"Well," the chief said, sitting back in his chair, "I'm afraid I'm going to have to ask you to leave Omaha."

"Excuse me?"

"You must admit, you have a reputation for attracting trouble."

"I'm not here looking for trouble," Clint said.

"I didn't say you were," the chief said. "But it's going to find you, isn't it?"

DON'T MISS THESE
ALL-ACTION WESTERN SERIES
FROM THE BERKLEY PUBLISHING GROUP

THE GUNSMITH by J. R. Roberts
Clint Adams was a legend among lawmen, outlaws, and ladies. They called him . . . the Gunsmith.

LONGARM by Tabor Evans
The popular long-running series about Deputy U.S. Marshal Custis Long—his life, his loves, his fight for justice.

SLOCUM by Jake Logan
Today's longest-running action Western. John Slocum rides a deadly trail of hot blood and cold steel.

BUSHWHACKERS by B. J. Lanagan
An action-packed series by the creators of Longarm! The rousing adventures of the most brutal gang of cutthroats ever assembled—Quantrill's Raiders.

DIAMONDBACK by Guy Brewer
Dex Yancey is Diamondback, a Southern gentleman turned con man when his brother cheats him out of the family fortune. Ladies love him. Gamblers hate him. But nobody pulls one over on Dex . . .

WILDGUN by Jack Hanson
The blazing adventures of mountain man Will Barlow—from the creators of Longarm!

TEXAS TRACKER by Tom Calhoun
J.T. Law: the most relentless—and dangerous—manhunter in all Texas. Where sheriffs and posses fail, he's the best man to bring in the most vicious outlaws—for a price.

THE GUNSMITH
367
THE OMAHA PALACE

J. R. ROBERTS

*Daniel Boone
Regional Library*

JOVE BOOKS, NEW YORK

THE BERKLEY PUBLISHING GROUP
Published by the Penguin Group
Penguin Group (USA) Inc.
375 Hudson Street, New York, New York 10014, USA

Penguin Group (Canada), 90 Eglinton Avenue East, Suite 700, Toronto, Ontario M4P 2Y3, Canada (a division of Pearson Penguin Canada Inc.) • Penguin Books Ltd., 80 Strand, London WC2R 0RL, England • Penguin Group Ireland, 25 St. Stephen's Green, Dublin 2, Ireland (a division of Penguin Books Ltd.) • Penguin Group (Australia), 250 Camberwell Road, Camberwell, Victoria 3124, Australia (a division of Pearson Australia Group Pty. Ltd.) • Penguin Books India Pvt. Ltd., 11 Community Centre, Panchsheel Park, New Delhi—110 017, India • Penguin Group (NZ), 67 Apollo Drive, Rosedale, Auckland 0632, New Zealand (a division of Pearson New Zealand Ltd.) • Penguin Books (South Africa) (Pty.) Ltd., 24 Sturdee Avenue, Rosebank, Johannesburg 2196, South Africa

Penguin Books Ltd., Registered Offices: 80 Strand, London WC2R 0RL, England

This is a work of fiction. Names, characters, places, and incidents either are the product of the author's imagination or are used fictitiously, and any resemblance to actual persons, living or dead, business establishments, events, or locales is entirely coincidental.

THE OMAHA PALACE

A Jove Book / published by arrangement with the author

PRINTING HISTORY
Jove edition / July 2012

Copyright © 2012 by Robert J. Randisi.
Cover illustration by Sergio Giovine.

All rights reserved.
No part of this book may be reproduced, scanned, or distributed in any printed or electronic form without permission. Please do not participate in or encourage piracy of copyrighted materials in violation of the author's rights. Purchase only authorized editions.
For information, address: The Berkley Publishing Group,
a division of Penguin Group (USA) Inc.,
375 Hudson Street, New York, New York 10014.

ISBN: 978-0-515-15101-5

JOVE®
Jove Books are published by The Berkley Publishing Group,
a division of Penguin Group (USA) Inc.,
375 Hudson Street, New York, New York 10014.
JOVE® is a registered trademark of Penguin Group (USA) Inc.
The "J" design is a trademark of Penguin Group (USA) Inc.

PRINTED IN THE UNITED STATES OF AMERICA

10 9 8 7 6 5 4 3 2 1

If you purchased this book without a cover, you should be aware that this book is stolen property. It was reported as "unsold and destroyed" to the publisher, and neither the author nor the publisher has received any payment for this "stripped book."

ALWAYS LEARNING   **PEARSON**

ONE

Ashley Burgoyne stared down at the naked man in her bed. He was in his twenties, muscular, handsome, well enough endowed to satisfy her—if he knew what to do with his asserts, which he didn't. And she didn't have the time to teach him. She had spent years as a whore, catering to the whims and wants of men. Now that she was older—not that thirty-five was old—and had her own place, she was determined that men were going to service her, not the other way around.

She reached down and took hold of his rigid cock. The skin was smooth and hot, he had good girth and fairly good length, but a man was more than a hard cock. This one had no idea what to do with his hands or his mouth. He was all cock. Stick it in and pump away, that was his style—and that just would not do.

"Just lie still," she said to him. "I can see I'm going to have to do all the work."

"But Ashley," he said, "I'll do whatever you want—"

"Maybe," she said, "but right now I just want you to lie still, precious, all right?"

She had never been a large woman, but she was a bit fleshier in her breasts and thighs these days. Despite that, she was still a beautiful, desirable woman, which was how she got young men like this one to submit to her.

She straddled him, reached down to hold his cock in place. Then slid down on him, taking him inside her hot, wet pussy. He gasped as her heat enveloped him, and he reached for her, but she slapped his hands away. He'd only annoy her.

"Lie still!" she said.

He did as he was told, and she began to ride him, taking her time, finding the right rhythm, okay, okay, there it was, that was good, but then after a while it wasn't getting any better. If he'd known how to move with her, it would have helped, but he was hopeless in that department.

She tried a bit longer, but she was getting only a certain degree of pleasure from this, and no more.

Finally, she dismounted and said to him, "That's it. Get dressed and get out."

"But Ash—"

"Just go . . ." She groped for his name but it didn't come. "Just go!"

Sadly, with a sullen look on his handsome young face, he got dressed and left her room. Ashley had no choice but to lie back and do the job herself. She reached down between her legs and began to touch, to rub, all the while thinking of Clint Adams . . .

* * *

Of course, she had been thinking about Clint Adams for days.

She had opened her saloon and gaming palace in Omaha, Nebraska, only about a week ago. The attendance since then had already indicated that Ashley's Palace was going to be a success, but she still had some ideas.

One idea was the huge opening party she was going to throw in a week. Even though she was already open, *that* would be the Grand Opening. She had invited every local dignitary she could think of, including the mayor. But the guest she wanted was Clint Adams, and any friends that he might be able to bring along, such as Bat Masterson or Luke Short.

So she'd sent telegrams all over the West, hoping that one would find him. Denver, Saint Louis, San Francisco, anyplace she thought he might be. Even to Labyrinth, Texas, which he had mentioned to her one time.

She wondered, if he came, what he would think of her after ten years. When she looked in the mirror, she liked what she saw, but would he? The Ashley—although that wasn't her name back then—that he remembered would be twenty-five years old.

She put the finishing touches on her black hair and stood up from her dressing table. She was wearing a lavender dress, low cut to show an appealing expanse of cleavage and shoulder. She knew when she walked through her place that she drew looks from the men, even with younger girls working the floor.

She went to the door and opened it, feeling only as slight

afterglow from servicing herself after her young man had flunked his test. Maybe she'd find another man tonight, perhaps someone older who knew how to please a woman.

That damn Clint Adams, though—ten years ago he had pretty much ruined her for any other man. Since then she'd never found anyone who made her feel the way he did.

TWO

Clint Adams rode into Omaha, Nebraska, three days before the big opening party at Ashley's Palace. Of course, he didn't know at the time there was to be a party. He was simply responding—as he often did—to a telegram asking him for help. This telegram was signed with a name he hadn't seen or heard in over ten years. The telegram had found him in Labyrinth, Texas. He had just ridden in from a few weeks on the road, so he packed some clean clothes and rode out again the very next day.

South Texas to Omaha, Nebraska, was a haul, and when he rode in, both he and Eclipse were dragging their asses. Council Bluffs, Iowa, was right across the river, and it had long been the jumping-off place for wagon trains traveling west. The first thing they had to do was dismantle the wagons so they'd float across the river to Omaha. There they'd have to stay awhile, get their wagons reassembled, get outfitted for the trip west. Omaha was a much larger city than it had been the last time he was there.

The hotel he had stayed in then was gone. The livery stable was still there, though, so he stopped there first. He didn't recall if it was the same man or not, but this one seemed sufficiently impressed with Eclipse, and Clint felt confident leaving the horse in the man's care.

"You know a good hotel?"

"We got lots of hotels, mister," the older man said. "Cheap or expensive?"

"Somewhere in the middle," Clint said.

"Try the Hotel Aksarben," the man said.

"Aksarben?" Clint asked. "What kind of name is that?"

The man laughed and said, "That's how you say Nebraska backwards."

"I guess that's kind of clever, then," Clint said.

He took his saddlebags and rifle and walked to the Hotel Aksarben. Along the way he got a look at the outside of Ashley's Palace. It had two stories, peaks on it like a palace, and a big balcony, the kind that could accommodate a lot of girls waving at cowpokes as they rode by.

The Palace was closed at that time of day, so he turned and went into the hotel to get himself a room.

By the time he had checked in, cleaned up in his own personal washroom, donned a fresh shirt, and gone back down to the lobby, the front doors of the Palace had opened.

The Aksarben was a modern hotel, with indoor facilities, but they hadn't gotten around to putting bathtubs in the rooms. There were, however, tubs available on the first floor. Clint would keep that in mind for later.

THE OMAHA PALACE

He stepped out of the hotel and looked across at the open doors of the Palace. The front windows were ornate, difficult to see through. He had a feeling that was deliberate. He crossed the street and walked up to the batwing doors, looked inside. There was a partition just inside, kept a body from seeing the interior. When you entered, you would have to walk around the partition to finally enter the saloon. The owner certainly didn't want anyone getting anything for free, and that included a look inside.

He stepped through the door, and around the partition. The inside was cavernous with high, chandeliered ceilings. The bar wasn't the longest he'd ever seen, but it was close.

There were no people except for those who worked there. A bartender was behind the bar, working on it with a rag. There was another man taking chairs down off the tables and setting them on the floor.

Clint walked to the bar, saw that the bartender was a man in his thirties, stood as comfortable as could be behind a bar.

"Kinda early," the bartender said.

"Doors are open."

"They are, and that's a fact."

"That's okay," Clint said. "I smell coffee. That'll do for starters."

"Comin' up," the bartender said, "and no charge."

"Why would that be?" Clint asked.

The bartender put a mug of coffee on the bar and shrugged. "Just too damn early to do business."

Clint stepped to the bar and picked up the hot coffee mug.

"Much obliged," he said.

"Just ride in?" the bartender asked.

"That's right." He sipped the coffee. Good and strong. He was able to tell that by the smell.

"Passin' through?" The bartender sipped his own coffee. The other man was making noise, dropping the chairs on the floor.

"Not really," Clint said. "I'm here looking for a friend."

"What's the fella's name?"

"Not a fella," Clint said. "A girl. Her name is—well, it was—well, her telegram said that her name is Ashley."

"Ashley?" the barman asked. "Our Ashley?"

"That's what I'm here to find out."

"Well," the man said, "she don't usually come down before the afternoon, but I could send Leo there upstairs to tell 'er you're here. What's your name?"

"Clint Adams."

"Adams?" the man asked, surprised. "You mean . . . the Gunsmith?"

"Yeah," Clint said, "that's what I mean."

"Well," the man said, "my name's Ed Wright. Happy to meet you."

They shook hands.

"Leo," Wright shouted, "leave those chairs. Go up to Miss Ashley's room and tell her Clint Adams is here."

Leo, a young man in his twenties, looked over at Wright and said, "She don't like bein' woke up."

"Just do it!" Wright yelled.

Leo slammed one more chair down on the floor, then trudged upstairs to deliver the news.

THREE

Ashley actually was asleep, having chosen the night before to sleep alone. When Leo pounded on her door, she came awake with a start.

"Who is it?" she demanded.

"Leo, Miss Ashley." The young man's tone was tremulous, as he was expecting her to react angrily.

"Whatayou want?"

"It ain't my fault," Leo said. "Ed sent me up to tell ya somethin'."

"Damn it," she said, "hold on."

She stood up, grabbed a nearby robe, put it on, and belted it as she walked to the door. She opened the door a crack so she could see Leo, but he could not see her face, which she had not had time to make up yet.

"What is it, Leo?" she said.

"Ed says there's a fella here to see you."

"What fellow?"

"Name of . . . Allan? I think?" Leo scrunched up his face. "I disremember . . ."

"Allan?"

"Clint Allan?"

"Do you mean Clint Adams?"

Leo's face brightened.

"That's it!"

"Well, why didn't you say so?" she demanded. "Tell Ed to give him a drink—or coffee—or something. I'll be right down. I've got to get dressed!"

"Yes, ma'am," Leo said. "Whatever you say."

"Go!"

Leo, who was hopelessly in love with Ashley, was not happy about her attitude toward this fella Adams.

Wait.

Clint . . . Adams?

That name was familiar . . .

"Here's Leo," Wright said. "You tell 'er?"

"Yes, sir," Leo said. "She says to give him a drink or somethin', and she'll be down soon."

"There ya go," Wright said to Clint. "I guess maybe she's the right Ashley?"

"I guess she is," Clint said.

"Warm that coffee up for ya?"

"Sure, go ahead," Clint said.

Ashley spent time picking out the right dress, getting her face just right. She was nervous because she hadn't seen Clint Adams in ten years. What was he going to think when he saw her?

THE OMAHA PALACE

She worked on her face with powder, and rouge, and red lipstick. Then she tried on half a dozen dresses before she found the right one. She usually didn't wear her gowns this early in the day, but she was hoping to hide the years beneath makeup and silk.

Lastly, she worked on her black hair, piling it up on her head, leaving her neck bare. Clint had always said he liked her neck, and she still felt that it was smooth and graceful.

Finally she stood in front of her freestanding full-length mirror, the one she had purchased back East and had shipped to Omaha. She turned left and right, hands on her waist, which was still rather trim. While she no longer had the body of a twenty-five-year-old girl, she hadn't been getting many complaints lately.

With butterflies in her stomach, she opened the door to her room and stepped out.

FOUR

"Here she comes," Ed Wright said.

Clint looked at the stairs but didn't see anybody.

"How do you know?"

Wright laughed.

"Oh, I can always hear her door close," Wright said. "And I can hear her footsteps."

Clint strained, but couldn't hear a thing.

"You must have very good hearing."

"It's just from habit," Wright said. "Ya gotta know when the boss is comin', ya know?"

"How long have you worked here?"

"Been here since she opened a few weeks ago."

"Did you know her before that?"

"Nope," he said. "She hired me when I came in to apply for the job as bartender."

"Are you more than a bartender?"

Wright smiled and said, "She kinda made me the manager, too. I got experience. Ah, there she is."

Clint looked up and saw a woman descending from the second floor. She took the stairs slowly, as if she was in no hurry. She was wearing a blue gown, low cut to reveal her shoulders and breasts, her lustrous black hair piled high on her head, revealing a long, beautiful neck.

When she got to the floor, she glided across the room and a smile spread across her lovely face.

"Clint," she said. "You came."

"Did you think I wouldn't?"

He took her in his arms, hugged her tightly. She was not the slender girl he had known ten years ago, but there was nothing wrong with the solid body he had in his arms.

She kissed him quickly, then asked, "Has Ed been looking after you?"

"He gave me some fine coffee."

"Is that all you want?" she asked. "We can give you something go eat, or something else to drink—"

"I'm fine, Ashley," he said, the name sounding odd to him. It wasn't the name he'd known her by.

"Well then," she said, "why don't we go to my office so we can talk?"

"All right."

She picked up a mug of coffee Ed Wright had poured for her and said, "Grab your coffee."

Clint did so, and followed her to the back of the room and into her office.

Once in the small but well-appointed room, she put her coffee down, took his from him and set it next to hers, then went into his arms again for a longer kiss.

"Oh, it's been a very long time," she said.

"Yes, it has," he said. "You are absolutely gorgeous, Ka— Ashley." He'd almost called her Kate, the name he'd known her by.

"Am I?" she asked. "I wasn't sure what you'd think after ten years."

"The years have not only been kind to you," he said, "they've been extremely kind. You were a pretty girl, but you are now a beautiful woman."

"That's such a relief," she said, "even if you're lying."

"I'm not."

She kissed him again, then slid from his arms and moved behind her desk.

"Sit, please," she said. "I know my telegram must have been confusing."

"A little," he said. "I read between the lines."

"Did you say anything to Ed?" she asked. "I mean, about what my name used to be?"

"No," he said.

"Good. I don't want my past showing up here."

"Quite a place you have here, Ashley," he said. "You must be doing very well to be able to open a place like this."

"I have investors, but yes, I am doing all right," she said. "We're having a grand opening in a few days."

"Haven't you been open?"

"Uh, yes," she said, "but I want to do it up right, you know? Have a big party."

"Sounds like fun."

"You'll be there, I hope."

"I guess that depends."

"On what?"

"On why you sent for me," he said. "On whether or not I'll still be here."

"I hope you'll be here."

"Why don't we get to the reason you sent for me?" he asked. "And then we can see."

"All right," she said. "I would like you to deal faro for me."

"I haven't dealt faro in a while, Ashley," he said.

"I think you probably still know how."

"I'm sure I do," he said, "but that's not usually a job I do."

"I understand that," she said. "But I'm trying to make sure my place gets off to a good start, and I think having the Gunsmith here, dealing faro, will do that."

Clint frowned.

"Okay," she said, "yes, I'm trying to use your name, and yes, I'm trading on our friendship. At least, I hope we're still friends after all these years."

"Of course we are," he said.

"But?"

"I just don't like the idea very much," he said.

"So you won't do it?"

"I didn't say that."

"Then you will?"

"Didn't say that either."

"Then what are you saying, Clint?"

"I think we should probably talk about it a little more," he said, "maybe tonight, over dinner."

"Still like steak?" she asked.

"I do."

"Then I'll get you the best steak you've ever had," she said, "and we can talk."

"That," he said, "I can agree to."

FIVE

Ashley admitted to Clint that she didn't usually get up this early.

"I'm not at my best," she added.

"You could have fooled me."

She took his arm and walked him out of her office and back into the saloon.

"Where are you staying?" she asked.

"Place called the Aksarben."

"Not the best hotel in town, but it's all right," she said. "You could stay here, you know."

"I don't think so, Ashley," he said. "At least, not yet."

"I understand."

When they reached the bar, Ed Wright grinned and said, "You two get reacquainted?"

"Get your mind out of the street, Ed," Ashley said.

"Hey, I didn't mean nothin'!" he said.

"Clint, I'll see you tonight for dinner. Pick me up here at six."

"I'll be here."

She turned to Wright and said, "Anything Mr. Adams wants here is on the house. Got it?"

"I got it, boss," Wright said.

Leo was still setting up chairs, and he tossed a resentful look at Clint.

"And that includes the girl," she added. She looked at Clint. "We've got some pretty ones here."

"I don't think I'll even notice them with you around," he said.

"You still know how to talk to a woman," she said. "My girls are going to love you. I just want you to know they're at your—"

"Don't worry about it, Ashley," he said. "I'll see you for dinner."

"Six," she reminded him, and then went back up the stairs to her room.

Clint looked at Wright and asked, "Who's the law in Omaha?"

"Sheriff, or police?" the bartender asked. "We got 'em both."

Clint made a face. He didn't want to have to deal with a police chief.

"I'll settle for the sheriff."

"Don't blame ya," Wright said. "His name's Thorpe, been sheriff here for a couple of years."

"Thorpe," Clint said. "Don't know him. I guess I'll go over and introduce myself."

"He's an okay fella," Wright said.

"Known him for a while?"

"I been in Omaha five years," Wright said. "I know most folks."

"Thanks for your help, Ed," Clint said. "I'll see you later."

"Sheriff's office is outside to your right, two blocks. Can't miss it."

"Thanks, Ed."

Wright was correct—Clint couldn't miss the sheriff's office. There was a shingle in front of it that said IAN THORPE, SHERIFF sticking out on a post rather than hanging on the wall.

He started to turn the knob and go in, thought better of it, and knocked.

"Yeah, come in!" a voice called.

He opened the door and entered. The office and the man inside had the same look of neglect. The desk was old, the potbellied stove older, and the man behind the desk had seen better days. His clothes were rumpled, his eyes red-rimmed, and Clint had an idea that what was in the white coffee mug was not coffee.

"Knew it was a stranger," the sheriff said.

"How'd you know that?"

"Nobody around here knocks first," the man said. "What can I do for you?"

"Are you Sheriff Thorpe?"

The man brushed aside his vest to show the badge pinned to his shirt.

"That's me."

"My name's Clint Adams, Sheriff," Clint said. "I just

arrived in town about an hour ago. Thought I'd stop in and let you know."

Thorpe sat back in his chair and stared at Clint.

"Why stop in here?" he asked. "Omaha's got a brand-new police station, complete with a brand-new police chief. So why me?"

"I'm still a firm believer in the local sheriff," Clint said. "As far as I'm concerned, police departments can stay in the East."

"You and me both, friend," Thorpe said. "Would you like a drink?"

"No thanks," Clint said. "Too early for me."

"Used to be too early for me, too," Thorpe said, "but those days are gone."

To illustrate his point, he took a bottle of whiskey from his bottom drawer and poured a few dollops into his coffee mug.

"What brings the Gunsmith to town?"

"Visiting a friend."

"Oh? Who's that?"

"Ashley, of Ashley's Palace."

"Fine-lookin' woman," Thorpe said. "Got herself quite a place there."

"Yes, she has."

"Gonna help 'er with it?"

"Don't see that she needs much help," Clint said. "We're just catching up. It's been a while."

"Well, I appreciate you comin' in here to let me know you're in town," Thorpe said. "But you want some advice?"

"Sure."

"Take you a walk over to the police department and let the chief know you're here."

"Why's that?"

"He's the one folks around here answer to when there's trouble," Thorpe said. "He's got a brand-new building, all fresh and clean." Thorpe waved an arm. "You can see what I got. I'm not even sure I can find the key for the cells."

"Well, I'm not looking for trouble," Clint said. "And if I run into any, I'll just mention your name."

Thorpe laughed.

"Fat lotta good that'll do you, but be my guest. See how much good it does ya."

Thorpe went back into his cup and Clint left him there.

SIX

Clint left the sheriff's office and walked along aimless for a while after that. He eventually came to the new police department building, saw what the sheriff had meant. It did look clean and new, a two-story brick building that seemed to be the model for new Eastern-style police departments that were popping up in the West.

He considered going inside, but he'd recently had dealings with police chiefs and police departments that he wasn't thrilled with, which explained why he still preferred the old position of town sheriff.

He headed back to his hotel, and along the way he noticed the kid, Leo, from Ashley's Palace going into a smaller saloon that looked like it belonged to the old Omaha. He had a feeling this would be the kind of place Sheriff Thorpe drank in.

He walked past it, giving it just a glance. If he'd been in

the mood for a beer, he would have gone inside, but instead he just kept on walking toward his hotel.

Leo stood at the bar, ordered a beer, and proceeded to complain about Clint Adams.

Eventually, he had placed the name, but he wasn't so impressed with the old-time gunfighters, like most people were. They were part of the past, and pretty soon they'd just disappear.

The bartender poured the kid a drink and said, "The Gunsmith's in town?"

"Yeah, he is."

"Where'd you see him?"

"Ain't you been listenin', Bull?" Leo asked. "I saw him over at the Palace."

"What's he doin' there?" Bull asked.

"Looks like he's friends with Miss Ashley," Leo said sourly. "Don't know what she sees in such an old guy."

"An old guy with a reputation," Bull said. "And he ain't so old."

"He's gotta be over forty!" Leo complained.

Bull, who was forty-five, said, "That ain't so old, kid."

Leo was not convinced.

At a table in the back of the small saloon, two men sat, listening to the kid's complaints.

"You hear what that kid's sayin'?" Casey Deal asked his friend.

"I hear 'im," John Rosa said. "What about it?"

"The goddamn Gunsmith is in town," Deal said. "You don't think the boss'll wanna know that?"

THE OMAHA PALACE 27

Rosa shrugged and said, "Yeah, I guess."

"Well, we're gonna be the ones to bring him the information," Deal said. "Finish your drink."

"I just got it," Rosa complained.

"Well, finish it!" Deal said. "The boss is gonna wanna know this right away."

"Why?" Rosa whined.

"Because the Gunsmith was in Ashley's Palace," Deal said. "Whatayou think that means?"

"I dunno," Rosa said. "Maybe he was thirsty."

"Yeah, and maybe he's gonna work there."

"As what?"

"Who cares?" Deal asked. "If word gets around that the Gunsmith works at the Palace, people are gonna flock to the place. Drink up."

Rosa downed his drink and both men stood, but as they started to leave the saloon, Deal made another decision.

"Come on, kid," he said, grabbing Leo by the back of his shirt, "you're comin' with us."

"Wha—"

"Hey!" Bull yelled.

"Don't worry about it, Bull," Deal said. "We won't hurt your little buddy."

They dragged Leo outside and stopped in front of the saloon.

"Whataya want?"

"I wanna know what the Gunsmith is doin' at the Palace," Deal said. "Tell me."

"All I know is he's friends with Miss Ashley," Leo said.

"And is he gonna work for her?"

"I dunno."

"Come on," Deal said, "there's somethin' else you know."

"Only that they're gonna have supper together later."

"Where?"

"I dunno, but he's supposed to meet her at the Palace."

"When?"

"Around six."

"Okay," Deal said. He drew his gun and stuck it in Leo's ribs.

"You said you wasn't gonna hurt me," Leo said.

"And I won't," Deal said, "but as soon as I hear you opened your mouth, I'll find you and kill you. Understand?"

"Y-Yeah, I understand."

"Just keep quiet about talkin' to us," Deal said, "and live. You wanna live, don't ya?"

"Yeah, I do."

Deal holstered his gun.

"Go back inside and finish your drink."

Leo went back in.

"Now what?" Rosa asked.

"Now," Deal said, "we go and talk to the boss."

"You think the kid'll really keep quiet?"

"He's scared enough," Deal said. "If not, he's a dead man."

Leo went back inside to the bar.

"What happened?" Bull asked. "What did they want?"

"Nothin'," Leo said. "They didn't want nothin'." He picked up his drink with a shaky hand.

SEVEN

Clint went to his hotel and made use of the bath facilities. If he was going to have supper with a beautiful woman, he didn't want to smell like a horse on the trail. After the bath he found a barber and had a shave and a haircut. With all of that done, he stopped and got himself some new clothes.

Sartorially resplendent, he presented himself at Ashley's Palace at five minutes to six.

"You smell real nice," Ed Wright, the bartender, said to him.

"Never mind," Clint said. "Just let me have a beer."

He drank his beer while looking the place over. It was doing a brisk business.

"How many other saloons are there in town?" he asked Wright.

"There are a few, but there's only one we have to worry about."

"You mean, for competition?" Wright nodded. "Which one's that?"

"Big Jack's."

"That's the name?"

"Big Jack's Saloon," Wright said, "owned by Big Jack Mackey."

"How long has he been in business?"

"A few years."

"So he doesn't like the competition?"

"Accordin' to him, everybody's welcome, but Big Jack's got his own ways of doin' things."

"Has he met Ashley?"

"He came by to talk to her a couple of weeks ago."

"And what did he say?"

Wright shrugged. "She don't tell me."

"But you're the manager, right?"

"When she lets me be. She's a real strong woman."

Clint was about to say more but at that moment the real strong woman approached them.

"Ready to go?" she asked.

"You look lovely."

"Thank you."

She had dressed down for supper, no flesh showing, although the dress was tight enough to show all of her womanly curves.

"Mind the store, Ed."

"Yes, ma'am."

"We'll be a Delfino's Steak House."

"Yes, ma'am."

She linked her arm in Clint's and they walked out the door.

* * *

At a table not far from the bar, both Deal and Rosa watched. Their boss had told them to find out for themselves, and not to take the word of a loser like Leo.

"Well," Rosa said, "I guess that settles it. They know each other."

"Pretty well, from the way it looks," Deal said. "But we still don't know if he's gonna work there."

"So how do we find out?" Rosa asked.

"Well," Deal said, "I guess the easiest way to find out would be to ask."

"Ask who?"

"Who talks more than anybody else in a saloon?" Deal asked him.

They both looked at the bartender.

EIGHT

Ashley led Clint to Delfino's, a large restaurant with a huge window in front. Ornate lettering spelled out the name of the place, both above the door and on the window.

"Best steak in town," she promised him.

"We'll see."

They entered and she was greeted at the door by a middle-aged man in a black suit.

"Miss Burgoyne," he said. "How wonderful to see you."

"Thank you, Dennis. A table for two, please?"

"Of course, of course, we have a lovely table by the window—"

"Something in the back, please," Clint said.

"Of course, sir. This way, please."

They followed him past occupied tables to an empty one in the back of the room. No one reached out for or spoke to Ashley, but Clint noticed that she drew the eyes of most of the men in the place.

"Thank you, Dennis," she said as he held her chair.

"I will send your waiter right over," he promised.

"Thank you," Clint said.

A waiter came over immediately and Clint allowed Ashley to order for them. She made it simple. Two steak dinners and beer.

While they waited, she asked, "Have you thought about my offer?"

"It was an offer?" Clint asked. "I thought it was a favor."

"Oh, all right," she said. "Have you thought about my favor?"

"I have," Clint said. "But first tell me about Big Jack."

"How do you know about Big Jack?"

"I've kept my ears open since I got to town," Clint said. "I heard he came to see you."

"He did," she said.

"What did he have to say?"

"He said I wouldn't last a month," she said. "He said I should enjoy my opening night party because things were really going to get bad from that point forward."

"So he threatened you."

"In a very charming way, with a smile on his face the whole time."

"Okay," he said, "tell me how long you want me for."

"Well, since he expects to close me down in a month, I'd say at least . . . six weeks?"

"And I get to keep what I win?"

"Definitely."

"Well," he said, "it's been a while since I dealt faro, but this sounds interesting."

"So you'll do it?" she asked.

The waiter came with their meals, and Clint said, "Why don't we leave it up to the steak? If it's good, I'll stay."

"You're kidding," she said.

"Hey," he said, "you told me how good it was. Don't you trust your own taste?"

She looked nervous as she said, "Well, of course I do."

"So it's agreed?"

She swallowed and said, "Agreed."

She watched with interest as Clint carefully sliced off a hunk of steak, examined it, and stuck it in his mouth. He followed it with a forkful of vegetables, and then chewed carefully.

"Well?" she asked. "What do you think?"

Clint made her wait until he'd swallowed before he answered.

NINE

Ashley had been waiting for Clint Adams for a long time. Once she got him in her bed, she knew the wait had been more than worth it. She would not only have a big-name faro dealer for at least six weeks, but enjoy an expert lover who knew how to treat a woman.

She reached down for his head and pressed her thighs to his ears . . .

When they got to Ashley's room, she was all over Clint, which he didn't mind at all.

"I've been waiting for this," she said, tearing at his shirt.

They undressed each other, and he was happy with what he found. She had put on weight from when he'd seen her last, but that just gave her beautiful big breasts and an ample butt for him to enjoy.

When they were naked, they fell onto her bed together, and she was ravenous. After a long, passionate kiss, he slid down between her legs, finding her wet and ready. She gasped when his mouth fell on her, and she grabbed his head and tightened her thighs on him.

"She went upstairs with him," Rosa said.
"Yes, she did," Deal said. "I think we found out what we need to know. Come on."
The two men got up and left the Palace.

When Rosa and Deal entered Big Jack's Saloon, they were immediately jostled by the crowd. Men were packed in at the bar, and all the seats at the gaming tables were occupied. Would-be players were standing, watching, and waiting for their turn.

"I'll go and talk to the boss," Deal said.
Rosa nodded. He didn't mind letting Deal do the talking with the boss. Big Jack intimidated Rosa, and he didn't like it.
Deal walked to the back of the noisy saloon and knocked on his boss's door.
"Come in!"
He entered, saw Big Jack seated behind his desk. Standing next to him was Janice, who was in charge of all the saloon girls. She was not beautiful, but she was smart and she had very large breasts, which Deal liked in a woman.
"Deal," Big Jack said. "Okay, Janice. We'll finish this later."
"Sure, Jack." She pressed her hip to her boss's shoulder before leaving, without giving Deal a look. Her day would come, Deal thought. He knew he'd get her naked one day.
"Put your tongue back in your mouth," Big Jack said. "What have you got for me?"

"They went out to eat, came back, and went right to her room."

"She took Adams to her room?"

"Yes, sir."

"Then she's sleeping with him," Big Jack said. "That might keep him here awhile."

"Yes, sir."

"I want to know what else he's doing for her. Most likely it'll have something to do with cards. You men keep watching."

"Yes, sir."

"And come and tell me as soon as you know something," Big Jack said. "Go on, get out."

Deal nodded, and left.

Outside Rosa asked, "What do we do?"

"We go back to the Palace," Deal said, "and keep watching."

"What fer?"

"He wants to know what else the Gunsmith is doin'," Deal said.

"Crap," Rosa said. "I'd rather stay here—I saw Janice come out after you went in. She's lookin' good."

"Yeah, she is," Deal said.

"She talk to you?"

"What would she wanna talk to me about?" Deal asked. "I was there to see the boss. Come on, let's go."

Rosa cast one more glance at Janice as she and her generous bosom went back into the boss's office.

"I don't like those two," she said as she came into Big Jack's office again.

"Don't worry about them," he said. "They're serving a purpose."

"Like I do?" she asked.

He smiled at her and said, "They don't serve anywhere near the purpose you do, sweetie."

She smiled back, tugged the top of her gown down so that her big breasts bounced into view.

"Come here," he said.

She moved around to his side of the desk, and he immediately seized both her breasts, squeezed them, and brought them to his mouth.

TEN

Big Jack sucked Janice's nipples while she moaned and cried out, then he took hold of her and laid her on his desk. He stripped her of her clothes until she was completely naked, then took off all his clothes while she watched, one hand busy between her legs. One of the things he liked about her was that she was completely uninhibited, easily the dirtiest woman he had ever known when it came to sex. She did everything and anything that he wanted.

All he wanted at the moment, though, was to climb on the desk and stick his dick in her. She had used her own fingers to get herself wet for him, and he slid into her very easily, despite his size. She gasped as he entered her, and then he began to fuck her. The desk was oak, thick and strong and able to hold the weight of both of them, even as they bounced around on it.

This wasn't the first time they'd fucked on his desk, and it wouldn't be the last.

Not hardly . . .

* * *

Clint was surprised at how different Ashley was from the girl he'd known, but then a lot of time had gone by. She'd grown into her body, which he had always known she would, and she'd had plenty of experience along the way.

He licked her pussy until she almost screamed, then he drove himself into her, enjoying the way her large breasts bounced as he did so. She closed her eyes, tossed her head back and forth on the pillow as he took her in long, hard strokes, and then suddenly she opened them, looked at him, and reached up. She pulled him down on her, then used her strength to roll them over so that she was on top. She managed to do it without forcing them apart.

When she had the superior position, she sat up on him and began to ride him. This was something she hadn't done ten years ago—she hadn't known enough, or had the strength, to exert her own will.

"Damn it," she said, grounding her crotch down on him, taking him as deeply inside her as she could, "if you only knew how long I've been waiting for this."

"I may be mistaken," he gasped, "but I'd say ten years."

She laughed, leaned down, and kissed him soundly, then sat up again and began to move up and down on him . . .

Big Jack knew his desk was jumping off the floor as they fucked, but he knew that even if someone outside the room heard that, they'd never come in. If they did, they'd be fired or, worse, shot.

"Oh God . . ." Janice gasped.

Abruptly, he withdrew from her, got down off the desk, and stood at the edge. He grabbed her legs, pulled her to the edge, then turned her over. She knew what he wanted, and didn't resist. From that position, he spread her considerable ass cheeks, pressed his hard cock to her anus, and then pushed it in. He did so slowly, until he was fully inside her, and then began to fuck her that way.

"Oh, yes, yes," she cried, "ooh, harder, come on, harder..."

He liked this position, but she was the only woman he'd ever been with who seemed to like it, too. The others had always been whores, and he'd always had to pay extra, but not with Janice...

She liked everything that he liked, and more...

ELEVEN

"When do I start?" Clint asked as they got dressed.

"Come by tomorrow morning," she said. "We can get you set up at a table."

"And when is the opening night party?"

"Three days."

As he pulled on his clothes, she donned a new dress, a low-cut green one she'd wear for the night in the saloon.

"And since you're working for me," she added, "check out of the hotel. I can put you in a room tomorrow as well."

"Okay," Clint said, "that'll work."

She took a deep breath, smoothed down her dress, and asked, "How do I look?"

"Gorgeous."

"Thank you. Would you like a nice cold beer?"

"I sure would."

"On the house, of course."

"Of course," he said.

"Come on," she said. "I'll introduce you to the others."

They went downstairs.

Big Jack picked up everything that had been knocked off his desk while Janice got her clothes back on. Then he got dressed.

"Time for you to go back to work," he said to her. "I have things to do."

"Yes, boss."

She went out the door, and he sat down behind his desk. Ashley's Palace's opening party was three days away. By then he wanted to know everything he could about her—and now, everything he could know about her relationship with Clint Adams.

Clint and Ashley went downstairs, where business was brisk, but could be better.

"There's still a lot to be done," she said to him as they walked to the bar. "But this place will soon be full every night."

"You've done a good job here, Ashley."

"Have I?" she asked. "I'd like you to say that after you've been here a few days, after you've seen my own operation."

"Is that part of my job, ma'am?"

"Part of the favor."

"Okay."

They reached the bar, and Ashley said to Ed Wright, "Two beers, Ed."

"Comin' up, boss."

"Make that three," she said. "One for you."

"Yes, ma'am."

He brought the three beers.

"What are we celebratin'?"

"Clint has joined us," she said, handing Clint his beer and picking up her own. "He's gonna be dealin' faro."

"Well, all right," Ed said. "When does he start?"

"Tomorrow."

"So when do I start puttin' the word out, boss?" the bartender asked.

"Right away," Ashley said. "Right after this beer."

They all drank their beers down, and then Ashley took Clint's arm and started introducing him to the others—the girls, the dealers, the security men.

Meet the Gunsmith.

TWELVE

The next morning Clint checked out of his hotel and carried his belongings over to the Palace. Ed let him in and showed him to his room.

"Come on down when you're ready," he said. "I'll have breakfast ready. Steak and eggs okay?"

"Great," Clint said.

"Strong, black coffee, right?"

"Right."

Ed withdrew, pulled the door closed behind him. The room was the size of a regular hotel room, furnished about the same way. None of the lavishness that existed in Ashley's room, but then he didn't need that.

He tossed his saddlebags onto the bed, and they bounced nicely. His stomach was growling so he didn't wait any longer. He went downstairs to have his breakfast.

* * *

Whoever did the cooking in the Palace's kitchen did a fine job. The steak was almost as good as the one he'd had the night before, the eggs were done just right, and the coffee was black and strong.

"You the cook?" he asked Ed Wright.

"Not me," Wright said. "Old Man Brennan makes that old stove sing."

"Old stove?"

"Best kind, he says," Wright replied. "Miss Ashley offered to buy him a new one, but he said he wanted an old stove, so that's what she got him."

"She must have a few investors to be able to afford this place."

"I don't concern myself with where the money comes from," Wright said. "I'm just happy it's there."

"How do you think this place will do against Big Jack's, Ed?" Clint asked.

"You been to Big Jack's?"

"I haven't."

"I think maybe you better go have a look," Wright said, "and then you can answer your own question."

"I think I'll do that," Clint said, "right after breakfast."

"They won't open their doors until noon," Wright told him.

"Well then, there's no hurry," Clint said, grabbing the coffeepot. "Might as well have some more coffee."

Clint was finishing up his coffee when Ashley came down. The bartender had finished his breakfast, cleared his place, and was behind the bar, where he knew his boss liked to see him when she came down.

"Coffee?" Clint asked her.

"Please."

He poured her a cup, and as he did so, an older man wearing a white apron came out from the kitchen with a plate of eggs for her.

"Thank you, Mike," she said. "Clint, Mike's my cook. Mike Brennan, this is Clint Adams. He'll be dealin' faro for us for a while."

"I heard," Brennan said. "Glad to have ya, sir."

"That was a fine breakfast, Mike," Clint said. "I don't see any reason to go anywhere else while I'm here."

"If you let me know what you want each night, sir, I'll have it waitin' for you in the mornin'."

"Steak and eggs are fine with me every morning, Mike."

"Yes, sir."

He went back to the kitchen.

"How'd you find him?"

"Same way I found Ed," she said. "He came in and applied for the job. I had him cook me breakfast, and then I hired him."

"Is that the way you hired everybody?" he asked. "The girls, the dealers . . ."

"Yes, why?"

"Are you sure none of them were sent over by Big Jack?"

"To spy, you mean? I'm fairly sure, but I can't be certain."

"Who's in charge of your security men?" Clint asked.

"I am," she said. "It's just two men with rifles to keep me from being robbed."

"You need somebody in charge, Ashley," he said, "and you need more than two men. You also need men you can trust."

"How do I know I can trust them?"

"Whoever you put in charge should hire them, only after he knows he can trust them."

"Would you do that for me, then?" she asked. "Who would know better than you?"

"I tell you what I'll do," he said. "I'll hire five men I like, and then I'll put one of them in charge. That way when I leave, you won't have an opening."

"All right," she said. "Thank you."

"I'm going to take a walk over to Big Jack's when it opens."

"What for?"

"Just to take a look at the competition," he said. "Maybe meet the boss."

"You can meet him the night of the opening," she said.

"You invited him?"

"Well, of course."

"That was a good move."

"I thought so," she said. "I'm not as dumb as some people think."

"I don't think you're dumb."

"No, no, I know that," she said, "and I'll be very happy to take advantage of your experience while you're here."

He raised his cup to her and she responded in kind.

"It'll be my pleasure," he said, "to supply it to you."

THIRTEEN

Clint waited until about twelve thirty to walk down to Big Jack's Saloon, having obtained the location from Ed Wright.

When he entered, the place was almost empty, except for a couple of men who looked like regulars with their tables staked out.

There was a lot of oak and gold leaf, some chandeliers. The place was impressive looking, but Clint thought Ashley had managed to get the upper hand as far as appearance was concerned.

He walked to the bar, where a bartender wearing a vest and a white shirt stared at him.

"Sir?"

"Beer, unless it's too early."

"If it's not too early for you, sir," the man said, "it's not too early for me."

He drew Clint a frothy beer and set it on the bar in front of him.

"Thanks."

"Haven't seen you in here before, sir."

"Haven't been in before," Clint said. "Been doing my drinking at the Palace."

"The new place," the bartender said. "Nice, but . . ."

"But what?"

"The lady running it really has no idea what she's doin'," the man said. "Now my boss, he's been in this business a long time."

"Is that a fact?"

"Jack Mackey," the bartender said. "Everybody just calls him Big Jack."

"Well," Clint said, "that must explain the name of the place."

The bartender frowned, like he was trying to decide if he was being made fun of.

Big Jack Mackey started every day the same way. He came down the back stairway from his rooms, entered his saloon by the back door, then opened the front door and stood in the doorway, looking his place over. His employees knew the place had better be spotless by then.

Now as he opened the door, he saw the man standing at the bar, talking to the bartender. When you ran saloons as long as he had, you tended to know on sight men who could handle themselves. Knowing that Clint Adams was in town, Big Jack thought he was putting two and two together and coming up with the right answer.

He decided to find out.

"Ah, here comes the boss now," the bartender said.

THE OMAHA PALACE

Clint turned, saw a tall, well-dressed gent with broad shoulders and graying hair. He looked to be in his mid-forties.

"Mornin', John," he said to the bartender.

"Mornin', boss," the bartender said. "New fella in town, checkin' the place out."

"That a fact?" Big Jack put his hand out. "Welcome to Omaha, Mr. . . ."

"Adams," Clint said, "Clint Adams."

"Ah, happy to meet you, Mr. Adams," Big Jack said while shaking hands. "I heard you were in town. Was hopin' you'd come and look at my place."

"It's impressive," Clint said.

"Thank you. I like it."

"All yours?" Clint asked. "Or do you have some partners?"

"No partners, no investors," Big Jack said. "It's all mine."

"Even more impressive."

"What brings you to town?"

"Came in to visit a friend of mine," Clint said.

"Oh? Anybody I'd know?"

"Maybe," Clint said. "Her name's Ashley Burgoyne."

"Oh, the lovely lady who owns Ashley's Palace," Big Jack said. "Have you known her a long time?"

"About ten years." He didn't bother to tell Big Jack that he'd seen her only one other time during those previous ten years.

"I understand this is her first saloon."

"That's true, but it seems to me she knows what she's doing."

"Well, for her sake, I hope so."

"And for your sake?"

Mackey smiled.

"I don't think I have to worry too much about her cutting into my business. Oh, maybe some in the beginning, but once the novelty wears off, the customers will come back here."

"Are you sure?"

"Very sure."

"So you'd have no reason to try to . . . sabotage her place?"

"Why would I do that?" Big Jack asked. "I just told you I wasn't worried. Is that why you came over here? To find out if I was threatened?"

"I'm new in town," Clint said. "I like to try out all the places in town before I pick my watering hole."

"You mean you won't automatically drink there?"

"I'll go where the best beer is," Clint said.

"Well then," Big Jack said, "get the man another beer, John . . . on the house."

FOURTEEN

Clint was still in Big Jack's when Sheriff Ian Thorpe came walking in and approached the bar.

"Hey, Sheriff," the bartender said. "Beer?"

"What else?" Thorpe asked sourly.

"Good morning, Sheriff," Clint said.

"Mr. Adams," Thorpe said. "Takin' a look at the competition?"

"Taking a look at the whole city, Sheriff," Clint said. "Quite a growth spurt since I was last here."

"Yeah," Thorpe said, accepting his beer from the bartender, "a growth spurt that includes squeezin' me out."

"That what they're trying to do?"

"Whether they're tryin' or not, they're doin' it," Thorpe said.

"Still got a year before elections, Sheriff," the bartender said. "Maybe things will change."

"I doubt that very much," Thorpe said. "Enjoy the city, Mr. Adams."

He took his beer and walked to a table.

"Does he spend much time in here?" Clint asked.

"Every day, pretty much," John said. "He's right, ya know. They're squeezin' him out, especially with the new police department."

At the mention of the new department, the batwings swung in and a young man in an Omaha Police Department uniform entered. He had a gun in a cavalry holster, and was carrying a nightstick. He headed directly for the bar, and Clint.

"Mr. Adams?" he asked.

"That's right."

"I'm Officer Brennan, sir," he said. "The chief would like to talk to you. He sent me to find you and ask you to come and see him."

"Ask, or tell, Officer?"

"He told me to ask you, sir . . . politely."

"I see."

"What can I tell him?"

"Why don't you just lead the way, Officer?" Clint said. "We can go see him right now."

"That would be very satisfactory, sir," the young officer said.

"Thanks for the beer," Clint said to John.

"Sure thing."

Clint looked over at Sheriff Thorpe, who silently raised his beer mug in a mock salute.

He followed Officer Brennan outside.

THE OMAHA PALACE

* * *

As they reached the new two-story brick police station—which looked like many of the others that had been popping up in the West—Clint said, "Brennan? Would you be related to a man who works at Ashley's Place?"

"He's my father, sir."

"Your father's a very good cook."

"I know that, sir."

"How do you feel about him working in a saloon?" Clint asked. "Is that a problem for you?"

"No, sir," Brennan said. "It beats what his previous job was."

"And what was that?" Clint asked.

Brennan looked at him, opened the front door for him to enter, and said, "He was the town drunk, sir."

Officer Brennan nodded to the sergeant manning the front desk and led Clint farther into the building. He was amazed that even the hallways seemed the same as police stations he'd seen in Denver, Salt Lake City, Cheyenne, Kansas City, and other places.

They reached an office that just said CHIEF OF POLICE on the door.

"Sir, Mr. Adams is here," Brennan said.

Clint was in the hall, didn't see the man who said, "Well, fine, bring him in," in a deep, bass voice.

"Mr. Adams?" Brennan said.

"Thank you."

"Mr. Adams?" the chief said as Clint entered. He was tall and reed thin, an appearance that did not jibe with his deep voice.

He extended his hand and Clint shook it.

"Have a seat."

Clint sat down. The chief seated himself behind his desk.

"Can I get you anything? Some coffee?"

"No, that's fine."

"I'd like to thank you for coming in," the chief said.

"No problem. I wasn't really doing anything else. What's on your mind, Chief?"

"Well," the chief said, sitting back in his chair, "I'm afraid I'm going to have to ask you to leave Omaha."

Clint stared at him and said, "Excuse me?"

FIFTEEN

"Don't get me wrong," the chief went on. "We like having new people come into Omaha."

"Except for me."

"Well, you must admit," the chief said, "you have a reputation for attracting trouble."

"I'm not here looking for trouble," Clint said.

"I didn't say you were," the chief said. "But it's going to find you, isn't it?"

"You don't know that for sure."

"Well . . . there are other reasons I can ask you to leave."

"Like what?"

"We have a vagrancy rule," the chief said. "If you don't have a job, you can't stay in town. And since you're just passing through—"

"Who told you that?"

"I beg your pardon?"

"Who said I was just passing through?"

"Well, I thought—"

"I have a job."

"Where, if I may ask?"

"Ashley's Palace."

"The new place," the chief said, nodding. "What will you be doing?"

"Dealing faro."

"And when did that start?"

"This morning," Clint said. "I was hired last night."

"Do you know Miss Burgoyne well?"

"I've known her for about ten years," Clint said.

"Well," the chief said, "it seems you've put me in an uncomfortable situation."

"You can't tell me to leave," Clint said.

"You did neglect to tell me you were in town," the chief said. "Don't you usually check in with the local law?"

"I did," Clint said. "I stopped in to see the sheriff when I got here."

"Sheriff Thorpe."

"That's right."

The chief frowned.

"You can check my story with both Miss Burgoyne, and the sheriff."

"I'm sure they'll back your story," the man said.

"It's not a story," Clint said. "It's what happened."

The chief was obviously at a loss.

"You mind if I go now, Chief?" Clint asked. "It is my first day of work. I'd hate to be fired for being late. That would make me a vagrant."

"Let me just warn you, Mr. Adams," the chief said. "At the first sign of trouble, I'll have you tossed into a cell."

Clint stood up and said, "I'll remember that."

He walked out of the office, unexpectedly ran into Officer Brennan, who was apparently waiting to walk him out. He followed the young policeman to the front door, neither of them saying a word.

Outside Brennan said to him, "The chief's kind of a hardnose."

"I guess so."

"He means what he says, though."

"Thanks for the warning."

"Yes, sir."

"I'll tell your dad that you're a respectful young man, and a good lawman."

"Thank you, sir."

Clint nodded and went down the steps.

He found a cab down the street and sat back after giving the driver the address of Ashley's Palace. The chief of police had managed to rub him the wrong way. He'd been warned by lawmen before, but one had never tried to drive him out of town on a whim, before anything had even gone wrong. The chief—obviously an Easterner—needed to develop some Western manners.

Brennan watched Clint Adams walk away, then went back into the building to the chief's office.

"Adams works in the same saloon your father works in, right?" the chief asked as Brennan entered.

"Yes, sir."

"I'm going to want you to keep an eye on him, Brennan."

"Yes, sir."

The chief stood up, came around from behind the desk. "I'm going out for some dinner."

"Yes, sir."

Brennan watched the chief go this time, was positive that the man was going to see Big Jack Mackey.

SIXTEEN

When Clint entered the Palace, he stopped first at the bar for a beer.

"You look mad," Wright said.

"I am." He told the bartender how the chief of police had tried to run him out of town.

"You ain't goin', are ya?" Wright asked.

"No," Clint said. "If I hadn't already decided to work for Ashley, he would have pushed me into it."

"Well, I'd keep an eye out for him and his men, if I was you," Wright said.

"Why's that?"

"He's supposed to have some kind of connection to Big Jack."

"Why doesn't that surprise me? Thanks." Clint picked up his beer and carried it to his faro table. He pulled the cover off and began to set his table up.

So the chief had tried to drive him out of town for Big

Jack Mackey? Looked like the law was in Big Jack's pocket. That would not make things easy. But then, when were they ever?

Big Jack entered the small, dark restaurant, saw the chief of police seated at a back table.

"It's about time," the chief said.

"Relax, Chief," Big Jack said, sitting down. "Don't flex your muscles at me. Save that for the Gunsmith."

"Yes, well, I tried that," the chief said. "It didn't work."

"Tell me."

The chief told Big Jack about his conversation with Clint Adams.

"And you let him talk to you like that?" he asked when the chief was done.

"What was I supposed to do?" the man said. "He hasn't broken any law, and he has a job."

"I want him out of town, Chief," Mackey said. "I don't want him working in that saloon."

"Now you relax," the chief said. "I haven't given up. At the first sign of trouble, I'll throw him into a cell."

"I want him out of town, not in jail."

"Well, once he's in my jail, I can get rid of him," the chief said. "It's up to you to make sure that trouble happens."

"Yes," Mackey said, "yes, I suppose I can take care of that. But I can't use any men who are already connected to me."

"So get some new men," the chief said. He waved to a waiter. "I'm ready to order."

"Enjoy your meal," Big Jack said, standing up.

"Not staying?"

THE OMAHA PALACE

"I'm particular who I eat with, Chief," Mackey said, and walked out.

On the street Big Jack put his hands in his pockets and started to walk. He wasn't in a hurry to get back to his place. He needed to do some thinking, come up with some names, and a plan. Probably the best way to get rid of Clint Adams would be to make sure he killed somebody. And if he was going to get some men to brace the Gunsmith, he was going to have to offer them enough money to make it worthwhile.

How much, he wondered, made it worthwhile for men to die?

The chief sat still while the waiter served him his chicken dinner. He'd managed to hold his temper in the face of Big Jack Mackey's insults. He usually did. Mackey's money made it worth it. And the chief had his own plans for Big Jack Mackey when the time came.

He cut into his chicken breast, found it moist, as usual. The chief usually got what he expected, and dealing with men like Big Jack Mackey and Clint Adams would be no different.

No different at all.

Clint stopped into the kitchen, where Old Man Brennan was getting his stove ready.

"Saw your boy today," he said.

"That a fact?" Brennan asked without turning.

"Yes. He seems like a fine young man. I'll bet he's going to be a good lawman."

"He is a good man," Brennan said. "Sure don't deserve an old man like me."

Clint didn't know what to say to that, so he turned and left the kitchen.

SEVENTEEN

When business started up that night, it was brisk from the get-go.

Apparently, the word had gotten out that the Gunsmith was dealing faro at Ashley's Palace. Men lined up to try their luck.

It hadn't been a long time since Clint had held cards. After all, he played poker very often. It had been quite a while, however, since he'd dealt faro, although it didn't take him long to get back into it.

Somewhere along the way he expected trouble. Either Big Jack or the chief himself would be sending somebody in to start something, maybe accuse him of cheating. All he had to do was stay alert. He wore his gun behind the table, but when the trouble came, he wouldn't be able to use his gun to handle it. Once he fired it, the chief would be able to justify putting him in a jail cell.

Clint had to find a way to recognize the trouble before it came, and handle it without drawing his gun.

Ashley came out of her office and liked what she saw. Business was booming—largely, she knew, because of the presence of Clint Adams.

She walked to the bar, where Ed Wright put a beer on it for her.

"How's he doin'?" she asked.

"He ain't losin'," Wright said.

"What about our other tables?"

"Not much goin' on there," Wright said. "They're waitin' in line to play him."

She looked at Wright.

"That's not good," she said. "I wanted to take in extra money by having people play him. I don't want them ignoring the other tables."

"Whataya wanna do, boss?"

"Get him to take a break and come to the office," she said. "We'll have to figure somethin' out."

"Want me to come, too?"

"No."

"But . . . I'm the manager, right?"

"Just do what I ask you to do, Ed," Ashley said. She picked up her beer and carried it back to her office.

Ed Wright came out from behind the bar and walked to Clint's table. He circled around and leaned over to speak into his ear.

"Boss wants you to take a break and go see her."

"Where?"

"Her office."

"Okay."

"Should I get somebody to spell you?"

"No," Clint said. "When I get up, they'll go to the other tables."

That was what the boss had said, Wright thought. Adams knew his stuff, but that didn't change the fact that Ed Wright was supposed to be the manager.

"Okay, folks," he said to the assembled men, "Mr. Adams is takin' a break, but the other tables are still open."

"When's he comin' back?" somebody asked.

"He ain't goin' nowhere," Wright said. "He'll be here all night. He's just takin' a break."

Clint covered his table, walked to the bar, and waited for Wright to get back behind it.

"Beer?" he asked.

"Comin' up."

Wright put the beer on the bar.

"You handled the crowd just right," Clint told him.

"Thanks. I wish the boss knew that."

"She probably does; otherwise why make you the manager?"

"Hey, she needed a manager," Wright said. "I was there. She still handles the day-to-day operations."

Clint sipped his beer, looked around at the two men seated in opposite corners of the room, with rifles across their laps.

"What do you think of the security guys?"

"Not much," Wright said. "If there's trouble, I think they'll just start shootin'."

"Without thinking?"

Wright nodded.

"We need thinkers more than we need shooters," Clint said. "Why don't we interview for some new men?"

"You want me to put the word out?"

"Sure, why not. And I'll want you to interview them with me."

"You throwin' me a bone?" he asked.

"You'll know the men we interview better than I will," Clint said. "Is that a problem?"

"Nope," Wright said, "no problem at all."

EIGHTEEN

Clint walked back to Ashley's office, knocked, and walked in.

"Have a seat," she said from behind her desk. "We need to talk."

"Yes, we do." He sat, holding his beer.

"You know what I'm going to say?"

"Long lines at my table, not enough players at the others."

"How do we change that?"

"Well, we can wait for the novelty to wear off."

"No good. What else?"

"I'm going to interview for new security men," he said. "I don't like the ones we have. I think we should have them work the floor, keep the aisles between tables clear. Tell the players they need to play where there are openings, and not all line up for the same table."

"You think that'll work?"

"I'll still have people at my table."

"Okay," she said. "When will you start interviewin'?"

"Tomorrow."

"Good."

"I'll want Ed to be there with me."

"Why?"

"Well, for one thing, he's supposed to be your manager," Clint said. "That means you should be letting him manage."

"And for another thing?"

"He'll know the men we're interviewing better than I do," Clint said.

"Good point."

"You have to give him more to do, Ashley."

"You're probably right," she said. "Okay."

"One more thing."

"What's that?"

He told her about his meeting with the chief of police.

"He tried to run you out of town?"

"That's right. And he didn't succeed. I also heard that he has a connection to Big Jack."

"You think Mackey put him up to it?"

"I do."

"So what's next?"

"They'll probably try to push me into doing something that will get me arrested."

"Like a fight in the street?"

"They might come in here and start something," Clint said. "Maybe accuse me of cheating."

"How do we avoid that?"

"We need good security."

"Well, you're going to take care of that tomorrow, aren't you?"

"I am."

"Then that'll be a good start."

"I better get back out there," Clint said. "We don't want to lose any of our players to Big Jack's place."

"Before you go . . . I was wondering if you . . . like your room?"

"I do."

"And your bed?"

"It's very nice."

"But mine's better," she said, arching her eyebrows. "You've already tested it out."

He turned to her and said, "Ashley, I don't think that would be such a good idea."

"Why not?"

"Because you're the boss."

"So? What's the point of being the boss if I can't have what I want?"

"Look," he said, "I thought you brought me here to help with your place, not warm your bed."

"You didn't object before."

"That was before you hired me. You're going to have to let me do my job, Ashley, and not expect me to . . . to perform for you."

She frowned, and he thought she was going to lose her temper, but to her credit, she didn't.

"All right," she said. "I see your point. But can I ask you one favor?"

"What?"

"Can you call me . . . Ash?" she asked. "Nobody does, and I kind of like it."

"I'll call you that when we're alone," he agreed. "How's that?"

"That's good," she said. "Now get your ass back out there to work before I fire you."

"Yes, ma'am."

As he opened the door and walked out, she came up behind him, caught the door before it closed, and watched him walk to his table. She also watched the other girls on the floor, watched how they watched him.

Had he found someone younger already?

Which one? she wondered.

NINETEEN

Leo watched Clint Adams go into Ashley's office, and then come out. He also saw her looking after him. He didn't like Clint Adams being here, didn't like the way she looked at him. But what could he do about it? The man was a gunfighter, and what was he?

But there had to be something he could do. He just had to be smart about it.

Karen Kearn also watched Clint as he walked back to his table. She was twenty-five, red-haired with freckles where a redhead should have freckles. She and the other girls had talked about Clint Adams, but none of them had really gotten to know him yet.

She was hoping she could change that tonight. As he sat back down behind his table, she started working her way over there. She darted away from grasping hands as she went, laughing and teasing. She was one of the more popular girls in the place.

Clint was back behind the table dealing when the redhead he'd been looking at all night came sidling up alongside him.

"Can I get you anything, Mr. Adams?" she asked, pressing her hip to his shoulder.

He looked up at her. "Karen, right?"

"That's right."

"I don't need anything right now, darling, but thanks for asking."

"I can come back later," she said, "and ask again."

"Later . . . when?"

She leaned over and said into his ear, "Later, like when we're both finished working?"

"That sounds interesting," Clint said. "But you'll have to call me Clint."

"I can do that . . . Clint."

"Hey," a sour-faced man who had been losing for hours asked, "are we playin' here?"

"We're playing," Clint said to him. He dealt out some cards, said, "You lose, friend."

"Shit!"

Clint looked at Karen again and said, "See you later, sweetie."

"All right," she said, and sashayed away.

Clint didn't know how Ashley would react if he slept with Karen, but the red hair and freckles were kind of hard to resist.

He went back to dealing.

THE OMAHA PALACE

* * *

By the end of the night Clint had gathered for himself a tidy sum. Turns out the very players who were anxious to play faro against the Gunsmith were also intimidated to play at the same table with the Gunsmith. For this reason they played badly, and lost . . . and lost . . . and lost . . .

Clint closed up shop, and covered his table, even though the saloon would still be open for a couple of hours, serving drinks.

He walked to the bar with his profits in one pocket, and Ashley's cut in the other.

"Beer," he said to Ed Wright.

"Comin' up." He set it down in front of him. "How was the action tonight?"

"Brisk," Clint said after a sip of beer. "There are a lot of bad faro players in Omaha."

"There are a lot of bad gamblers in Omaha," Wright said. "All of which is good for us, right?"

"Right."

Karen came to the bar to get a few drinks, then carried them off after giving Clint a hot look.

"Oh, my God," Wright said, "she is so pretty."

"Yes, she is."

"And she likes you."

"You think so?"

"Did you see the way she just looked at you?"

"Maybe you're right," Clint said as both men watched her walk away and serve the drinks.

"But you better watch out."

"For what?" Clint asked.

"The boss."

"What about her?"

"She don't like sharin'."

"She wouldn't be," Clint said.

"You mean you and the boss ain't . . ."

"She's the boss, Ed," Clint said. "That wouldn't be smart."

Wright leaned on the bar and asked, "Does she know that you and her ain't—"

"She knows," Clint assured him.

TWENTY

Ashley came out of her office as Ed Wright locked the front door. She converged with him and Clint at the bar. The two security men and their rifles had left earlier, which Clint didn't mind. They would not be back once he and Wright interviewed new men the next day.

Wright poured whiskey nightcaps for himself, Clint, and Ashley.

"By all accounts, your first night was a success," she said, raising her glass to Clint.

"Not for the players," Wright said with a smile.

"Can't tell anything from one night," Clint said.

They finished their drinks, set the empties down on the bar.

"I'll be working on the guest list for the party in the morning," she said.

"You still have Big Jack on it?" Wright asked.

"Definitely," she said. "He's been sending spies to look

my place over, so we might as well let him come in and have a good look himself."

"You know about his men coming in here?" Clint asked. He had noticed them more than once during the night.

"Oh yes," she said. "Ed?"

"Their names are Deal and Rosa," the bartender said. "He sends them in here all the time."

"I guess he thinks we don't see them," Ashley said.

"Don't kid yourself," Clint said. "He wants you to see them."

She looked at him in surprise.

"He's trying to make you nervous," Clint said.

"Well, he's not succeeding," she said.

"Good," Clint said. "I think it's a real good idea to invite him to the party. Let him know he's not making you nervous. But we're also going to increase our security."

"How?" she asked.

"I'll hire four men. They'll sit two on and two off, and they'll always have shotguns and pistols."

"Why both?" Wright asked.

"The shotguns are for show," Clint said. "We don't want them firing them off in a crowded saloon. Too many innocent bystanders will get hurt. If they have to use a gun, it'll be the handgun. So they'll have to be good with both."

"Well, you'd be the best judge of that I can think of," Ashley said.

"We'll get started early, Ed," Clint said.

"Sure thing."

"After breakfast," Clint added.

Wright grinned and said, "I'll tell Brennan to get it out early."

THE OMAHA PALACE

"Okay," Clint said.

"Well, boys," Ashley said, "I'm gonna turn in. I'll see you both tomorrow."

"Good night, boss," Wright said.

"Night, boss," Clint said.

"Good night."

They both watched her walk to the stairs and up until she was out of sight.

"You want some help cleaning up?" Clint asked.

"No," Wright said. "I'll just clean up the bar. Leo will come in and do the rest in the morning."

"What about Leo?"

"What about him?"

"He looks at me like he doesn't like me."

"Maybe he doesn't."

"Why wouldn't he?"

Wright hesitated, then asked, "You want a beer?"

"Sure."

He drew two and put them on the bar.

"Look," he said, "the boss, I guess you know she likes . . . well, men."

"Lots of women like men."

"Well, she likes 'em a lot, and she's tried out a few, but she can't seem to find one she really likes. You know?"

"Was Leo one?"

"No," Wright said. "She's had 'em young, but not that young. But he's in love with her, and he'd like to be one. I'm guessing he sees you as competition."

"Well, you tell him he's got nothing to worry about, okay?"

"Sure."

"I'm not looking to get shot in the back by some lovesick kid."

"Don't think he's got the nerve for that."

"That's good to hear. And what about you?"

"What about me?"

"Has she tried you out?"

"I've worked in a lot of saloons, Clint," Wright said, "and for some women bosses, and you know what I've learned. Don't sleep with the boss."

"That's a good lesson."

"Or the boss's wife."

Clint grinned and said, "That's even better."

TWENTY-ONE

Clint went to his room, and as expected, there was a knock at the door a short time later. He had removed his boots and shirt, washed up in the sink, and was about to start reading. He grabbed his gun from the bedpost and approached the door. He hoped it wasn't Ashley on the other side of the door. He didn't want to have to go through his explanation again. Sleeping with the boss just wasn't a good idea.

He cracked the door, saw red hair and freckles, and heaved a sigh of relief. He opened the door all the way.

"Come on in," he said to Karen.

She was still wearing her work dress, smelled pleasantly of perfume and a hint of girl sweat as she passed him.

"You were expecting me?" she asked.

"Wasn't I supposed to be?" he asked, closing the door.

"A girl doesn't like to be too predictable," she said. "But with a gun?"

"Don't be offended," he said. "I always answer the door with a gun."

He walked to the holster hanging on the bedpost and slid the gun in, then turned to face her. She walked to him, put one hand flat on his chest.

"Mmm," she said, rubbing her palm over his chest. "If we do this, will there be a problem with Ashley?"

"Does that matter?"

"I don't want to get into trouble with my boss," she said. "I don't want to lose my job."

"I'm with you on both of those things," he said, "so no, there won't be a problem with Ashley."

"Oh good," she purred. She slid both hands over his chest, up around his neck, and pulled him down into a kiss.

Jack Mackey opened the door to his house and said to Casey Deal and John Rosa, "Get in here quick!"

They darted in and he closed the door. He turned to face them, did not invite them any deeper into his home.

"How did the night go?"

"He had plenty of players," Rosa said.

"They was standin' in line," Deal said.

"Damn it," Big Jack said. "Did you hear what anyone was saying? What kind of dealer was he?"

"Well," Deal said, "nobody left his table with any money."

"They all lost?" Big Jack asked.

"All of 'em," Rosa said.

Big Jack shook his head. He hadn't yet decided what he was going to do. He might have to wait a few days to decide, maybe after the opening party.

"All right," he said, "get out."

"Do you want us to keep watchin' him?" Rosa asked.

"No," Big Jack said. "In fact, stay away from him. He's bound to have spotted you by now."

"He ain't seen us—" Deal started, but Big Jack cut him off.

"Stay away from him, understand?"

"Sure, sure, boss," Rosa said, "we understand."

"Then get out! Quickly!"

The two men opened the door and rushed out. Big Jack slammed it shut behind them.

He walked back into the house, saw Janice coming down the stars. She was wearing a filmy nightgown that trailed behind her. Her breasts and nipples were plainly visible through the fabric.

"What's wrong?" she asked.

"It was just those two idiots I had watching the Palace."

She came to him, put her hand on his arm.

"Is something wrong?"

"I don't know," he said. "It'll take me a few days to really decide."

Now she moved her hand to the front of his shirt, slid it inside to touch his skin.

"Why don't you come upstairs," she suggested. "I'll take your mind off all of this."

He looked at her and smiled, putting his hand over her breast.

"You will, too, won't you?"

"Oh, yes."

He cupped her breast through the thin fabric of her nightgown and rubbed the nipple.

"Come," she said. She slid her hand out of his shirt and took his hand. Without another word, she led him to the stairs and up to the bedroom.

Karen helped Clint out of his trousers, and stood still while he undressed her. Then he ran his hands over her body. Her flesh was smooth, firm, and hot, her breasts like ripe peaches. He thumbed her nipples until she sighed, then he gathered her into his arms for another kiss, their naked bodies pressed tightly together. She felt his hard penis between them and reached for it. She got down on her knees, took him in both hands, and sucked just the head, wetting it. She stroked the shaft and balls while she continued to suckle the spongy head, and then abruptly took him wholly into her mouth.

"Oh, God," he said, reaching for her. She tried to resist but he pulled her to her feet, then lifted her and dropped her onto the bed.

"Whoa!" she said as she bounced.

He got on the bed with her and kissed her neck, her freckled breasts, her belly, working his way down to the tangled red hair between her legs. When he plunged his tongue into her, she gasped and gathered up the sheet in her hands.

"Jesus . . ." She panted as he continued to lick her, enjoying her juices, which were both tart and sweet.

Suddenly she cried out, "Oh, God, yes!"

"Shhh," he hissed at her.

She put both her hands over her own mouth, then took them away and whispered, "I thought you weren't worried about the boss."

"Why take chances?" he asked.

That seemed to make sense to her, so from that point on, she bit her lip rather than cry out . . . and she did a lot of biting . . .

TWENTY-TWO

Clint came downstairs the next morning on rubbery legs. Karen was young, and it was all he could do to keep up with her.

"Breakfast?" Ed asked.

"Please. And plenty of coffee."

"Comin' up."

Clint sat down at a table while the kid, Leo, continued to take down chairs and set up tables.

Ed came out with two cups and a pot of coffee and sat opposite Clint.

"The old man will bring out breakfast," he said. "Steak and eggs."

"That's great."

"You look tired," the bartender said. "Didn't sleep well?"

"I slept okay . . . when I slept."

"Ah . . ." Ed said with a nod.

"Ah, what?"

"Never mind," the man said. "Not important."

The old man, Brennan, appeared carrying two steaming plates.

"Thanks, Mike," Ed said as he set them down.

Brennan grunted and went back to the kitchen.

Clint cut into his steak, picked up a chunk of it with some eggs, and forked it into his mouth.

"Today you'll go out and spread the word that we're interviewing men for a security detail," Clint said.

"What will you do?"

"I'll wait here for them."

"So I go out and collect and you stay here and interview?"

"That's the plan. You got a better one? After all, you know the men of Omaha better than I do. Send me the ones you think are capable and trustworthy, and I'll choose the four I think are best suited."

Ed shrugged and said, "Now that sounds like a plan to me, too."

They finished their breakfast, and as Ed Wright was leaving the saloon, Ashley came down the stairs.

"Where is he off to?" she asked.

"He's going to start picking out men for us to hire," he said.

"Mike!" she called out. "Breakfast!"

"Comin' up!" the old man called back.

She sat opposite Clint, and Mike Brennan brought out a cup and a fresh pot of coffee. He poured it out for both of them and then returned to the kitchen.

"How many men are you going to hire?" she asked him.

"Four."

"And how much will that cost me?"

"Don't forget," Clint said, "we'll be letting go the two men you have now. So it will only cost you for two more."

"And you think this is necessary?"

"I do, or I wouldn't do it."

"All right," she said. "I'll go along if you think it's right."

Brennan returned with a plate for her, eggs and bacon, but no steak.

"When will you begin interviewing men?"

"Anytime now," Clint said.

"Well," she said, "hopefully, I'll be able to finish my breakfast first."

Clint drank his coffee and sat with her while she ate.

"You know," she said, "I almost came to your room last night."

Happy she hadn't, he asked, "Why didn't you?"

"Because I thought you meant what you said," she answered. "And I think I need you more here in my Palace than in my bed . . . for now."

Good, Clint thought. They were on the same page. For all the assurances he'd given Karen that there would be no trouble with Ashley, he wasn't sure how she'd react if she had found him with the younger woman.

After breakfast Ashley told Clint she was going upstairs to get dressed.

"I'd like to see some of the men you hire," she told him.

"I'll run them all by you before we actually hire them," he said. "After all, you're the boss."

"Yes," she said, "I am."

He watched her walk up the stairs. When she was gone,

he cleared off the table, taking the remains of her meal to the kitchen.

"Here's the boss's plate," he told Brennan. "Where do you want it?"

The old man turned and, without a word, took the plate from Clint.

"You're welcome," Clint said, and walked out.

TWENTY-THREE

The first man came walking through the batwing doors, saw Clint seated at a table, and approached.

"You Adams?"

"I am."

"Ed Wright says you're lookin' for good men."

"He's right," Clint said.

"Whataya need 'em for?"

"He didn't tell you that?"

"Just that there was a job that needed good men," the man replied.

"We need some security for this place," Clint said.

"You expectin' trouble?"

"I am."

"From where?"

"Anywhere."

The man frowned. "What I mean is," he said, "you expectin' trouble from Big Jack?"

"Do you think I should be worried about him?" Clint asked.

"He don't like that this place opened," the man said.

Clint studied the man. He was in his thirties, wearing worn trail clothes and a well-used gun on his right hip. It was clean, though, and a man who kept his gun and holster clean always scored points with Clint.

"What's your name?"

"Gabe Falkner."

"Live in town?"

"I been around awhile," Falkner said. "Don't live here exactly. Got a room in a rundown hotel in the south end of town. Just not ready to move on."

"How much do you know about Big Jack?"

"Just what I hear," Falkner said.

"Do you know Big Jack?"

"No."

"So he didn't send you over here to get this job?"

"Naw," Falkner said, "I ain't never met him. But that would be a good idea, wouldn't it? I mean, on his part?"

"Yeah, it would." Clint studied the man again. For some reason, he believed him. Also, he had to take into account the fact that Ed Wright had picked him out.

"You drink here?" Clint asked.

"Usually."

"You can still drink here, but not on the job," Clint said.

"Sittin' around with a shotgun in your lap is dry work."

"An occasional beer," Clint said. "No whiskey. That okay?"

"That's fine."

"You got your own shotgun?"

"I do."

"You take as good care of it as you do your handgun?" Clint asked.

Falkner looked down at his gun, then said, "A clean gun is a happy gun."

"Okay," Clint said. "The pay is five dollars a week. And meals, if you want to eat here."

"Suits me," Falkner said.

"You know anybody else who might be a good fit? Or should I just count on Ed to send me the right men?"

Falkner shrugged and said, "He sent me in, didn't he?"

"You got a point there," Clint said. "Be back here at four with your shotgun. You'll meet the boss. She gets final say."

"She should," Falkner said. "She's the boss."

The man turned and left. Clint liked his attitude, and his comments. He hoped the man was as good as he was confident.

The second man came in about half an hour later, which suited Clint. Apparently Ed was taking his time choosing men to send in.

"What's your name?"

"Ben Atchison."

"Can you use that gun?" Clint asked.

"I can hit what I aim at."

"What about a shotgun?"

"What about it?"

"Can you use one?"

"Sure."

"Do you have one of your own?"

"No," the man said. "That gonna cost me the job?"

"No."

"What is the job?"

Clint explained.

"We gonna be goin' up against Big Jack?"

"Maybe," Clint said. "Is that a problem."

"Not considerin' I'll be on the side that's got the Gunsmith," Atchison said.

"You'll have to do your part."

"I'll hold up my end."

"Okay," Clint said. "Come back at four to meet the boss."

"Okay."

The man was in his late twenties, tall and gangly, with a heavy beard stubble.

"And get a shave and a bath before you come back."

"A bath?"

"A bath."

"Jeez . . ."

That was the only complaining he did. He turned and walked out.

While waiting for the next man to show up, Clint wondered idly what Big Jack would do if and when he heard that they were hiring. It *would* make sense for him to try to get a man in there. When Wright returned, Clint was going to have to ask him very bluntly how he'd found these men. If any of them had approached *him,* and not the other way around, Clint would have to look at that man a second time.

He stopped thinking about that when the third man came through the doors.

TWENTY-FOUR

The third man's name was Otto Gerald. He was not a gunman, but he was solidly built, knew how to use a shotgun and had his own. He was also older—in his fifties—and Clint liked that about him.

"You look like you can handle yourself," Clint said.

"Yeah," Gerald said. "I got big hands, and I know how to use 'em."

"So if we need some heads busted . . ."

"I'm your man."

"Okay, Otto," Clint said. "Be back here at four with your shotgun."

"Yessir. Thanks."

Clint sat back as Otto left, wondering who the fourth man would be.

About half an hour later Leo came through the doors. He had finished setting up all the chairs and had disappeared. Now he approached Clint.

"I wanna job as security," he said to Clint.

"Son, do you even have a gun?"

"I can get one."

"Do you know how to use a gun?"

"Whataya gotta know? Pull the trigger."

"Can you pull the trigger and kill a man if you have to?" Clint asked.

"Sure I can."

"I don't think so, Leo. You better stick to the job you've got."

"But I wanna—"

"It ain't going to happen, Leo," Clint said. "That's it."

Leo stared at Clint, then said, "I'll show you!" and stormed out. On the way he almost bumped into another man who was coming in.

"Whoa!" the man said as Leo went by. "Who set fire to his britches?" he asked Clint.

"I turned him down for the job," Clint said. "Are you here for that?"

"I am. Ed Wright sent me over."

This man was slick and handsome, looked like a gambler. In fact, he dressed like one, with a dark suit and a tie. But he wore a gun on his hip, and it was well cared for.

"You know how to use that gun?"

"I do."

"And a shotgun?"

"That, too."

"Got one of your own?"

"I do."

Clint sat back.

"You don't say much, do you?"

"I generally let my actions do my talkin'," the man said.

"What's your name?"

"Mike Lukas."

"Well, Mr. Lukas—"

"Mike," the man said. "Just call me Mike. And you're Clint Adams, right? The Gunsmith?"

"That's right."

"Well, I'm interested in the job," Lukas said, "whatever it is."

Clint explained the job to him and told him what it paid.

"That's okay with me."

"You sure?" Clint asked. "You don't look like a man who would work for five dollars a week."

"Five dollars is a lot when you've got nothin'."

"You gamble?"

"I do."

"Poker?"

Lukas nodded and said, "And the cards haven't been kind lately."

"It happens sometimes."

"Yeah, well, I guess you would know," Lukas said. "Do I get the job?"

"Come back at four with your shotgun. We'll see if the boss lady likes you."

"Thanks a lot," Lukas said. "I'll be here."

He turned and left. Moments later, Ed Wright came back in.

"I gotta get the bar ready," he said. "You get the men you need?"

"All four you sent in," Clint said. "But I've got to ask you something."

"What's that?"

"Did you approach all these men, or did one of them approach you?"

"Naw, I went to all of 'em," Ed said. "You said you wanted the best men we could find. These were them."

"Okay, then."

"You hired all of 'em?"

"I did, but the boss will have to look them over."

"She's gonna like Mike Lukas."

"I think you're right," Clint said, "but I hope she likes them all enough to let me hire them."

Wright went around behind the bar and started to set up for the day. Clint wanted some more coffee, but he didn't want to go into Brennan's kitchen.

"I'll be back in a while," Clint said. "The men will all be here at four, if the boss asks."

"Okay. Where ya goin'?"

"Just to get some coffee."

"Brennan in a mood?"

"Brennan's always in a mind, isn't he?" Clint asked. "At least, that's what I've been noticing."

Ed Wright laughed hard and said, "You been noticing right."

TWENTY-FIVE

Clint was drinking coffee, sitting at a table in an empty, nondescript-looking café, when Police Officer Brennan walked in. The young man stopped short when he saw Clint, then walked over to him.

"Hello, Officer Brennan," Clint said. "Are you looking for me?"

"No, sir," the young officer said, "this is just a coincidence. I came in to have some coffee."

"Well then," Clint said, "have a seat and join me."

Brennan hesitated, then said, "Yes, well, all right . . . thank you."

Brennan pulled out a chair and sat down. Clint called the waiter over and asked him to bring over another cup.

"Yes, sir," the man said, "right away."

As the waiter walked away, Brennan asked, "Can't you get coffee over at the saloon?"

"I could," Clint said, "but I'd have to ask your dad, and he's not in a very good mood."

"He's hardly ever in a good mood," Brennan said.

"Why is that?"

"Who knows?" Brennan said. "He's an ornery old man."

"So that sounds like you fellows don't get along."

"We haven't for some time, and probably never will," Brennan said.

The waiter came with the extra cup and filled it for the policeman.

"Thank you," Brennan said.

"Yessir."

The waiter withdrew.

"You mind if I ask you a few questions while you're here?" Clint asked.

"Why not?" Brennan said. "I still have an hour before I go on duty."

"What do you know about Big Jack Mackey?"

"What everyone knows," Brennan said. "He's a big man in Omaha, doesn't like competition, has political ambitions."

"Does he have guns in his employ?"

Brennan grinned. "What do you think? Don't men like him always have guns? Haven't you worked for men like him in the past?"

"We said I was going to ask you the questions," Clint reminded him.

"Okay. So what do you really want to ask about him?"

"What lengths will he go to to get rid of Ashley's Palace?"

"I don't think there's anything he wouldn't do," Brennan said. "Tomorrow night's the party, isn't it?"

THE OMAHA PALACE 105

"That's right."

"And everyone in town who is anyone is invited," the young policeman said.

"And you think he'll try something then?"

"With everyone in town on hand? Not likely. He'll be a perfect gentlemen, but he'll be looking for any sign of weakness. If I was you, I'd advise the lady to be on her best behavior."

"I'll keep that in mind. What's your chief's relationship with Big Jack?"

"I told you," Brennan said, "the man's got political ambitions. He knows the mayor, the chief, the town council, everybody. And the chances are he's got something on all of them. But you didn't hear that from me, right?"

"Right," Clint said.

"The word around town is you're hiring guns," Brennan said.

"We're hiring men for a security detail," Clint said. "Without guns, what good would they be?"

"What do you think Big Jack will do when he hears about it?"

"I don't know," Clint said, "but if the word is out, I guess he's already heard. If not, he'll see them tomorrow night at the party. Are you coming?"

"I'm not invited," Brennan said, "but the chief will be there."

"Maybe," Clint said, "I should go and talk to Big Jack again before the party. Just let him know where I stand."

"And where's that?" Brennan said.

"Right between him and Ashley's Palace."

"Well," Brennan said, standing up. "I just hope you've

got somebody you trust watching your back. Thanks for the coffee."

"Anytime."

As Officer Brennan left the café, Clint looked down at the policeman's cup and noticed he hadn't even taken a sip of his coffee.

Big Jack Mackey looked up as the man entered his saloon.

"Sorry to interrupt your breakfast," the man said.

"That's okay," Big Jack said. "It's my second one. Sit down."

The man sat.

"So what happened?"

"You were right," the man said. "The bartender, Wright, came to me."

"So you're in?"

"I will be, right after the boss lady meets me."

"When will that be?"

"We're all supposed to meet there at four."

"How many did Adams hire?"

"Four."

"The bartender got a gun behind the bar?"

"You ever know a bartender who didn't?" the man replied.

"And the old man?"

"He stays in the kitchen."

"He's the wild card in this business," Big Jack said. "Anybody know about him?"

"His son should."

"We might have to take care of him, but I'll know more after the party tomorrow night."

"You ain't gonna do nothin' until then?"

"No, and I don't want you to either. Just settle back and watch until you hear from me."

"Yessir."

When the man didn't leave, Big Jack asked, "Something else?"

"Well . . . you said something about . . . money?" the man said.

"Oh, yeah," Big Jack said. He took an envelope from his pocket and passed it over. "This is just a down payment."

The man looked impressed with the thickness of the envelope. He tucked it into his shirt.

"Thank you, sir."

"Now don't do anything until you hear from me, understand?"

"Yessir."

"Get out now."

The man nodded, stood up, and left. Big Jack went back to his second breakfast, was almost finished with it when another man walked in.

"Have a seat, Pete," he said.

Police Officer Pete Brennan sat down in the just vacated seat.

"You talk to Adams?"

"I did, sir."

Big Jack sat back. "Tell me."

TWENTY-SIX

Clint watched Pete Brennan come out of Big Jack's and walk down the street. Suddenly he had to take everything the young man said and view it with suspicion.

He crossed the street and entered the saloon.

"We ain't open yet!" the burly bartender said.

"It's okay, Dan," Big Jack said. "Mr. Adams is welcome."

The bartender frowned, but remained silent.

"Have a seat, Mr. Adams. Coffee?"

"No, thanks," Clint said. "I just had coffee with a friend of yours."

"Is that a fact?" Big Jack asked. "Who?"

"That's not important." Clint sat down. "A little late for breakfast, isn't it?"

"Actually," Big Jack said, "I'm such an early riser I have two breakfasts. What can I do for you, Mr. Adams?"

"I thought since the word seems to have gone out on the street, I should come and see you."

Big Jack wiped his mouth with a white cloth napkin, and sat back in his chair.

"Tell me what?"

"I've hired new security for the Palace," Clint said. "I'm going to make sure nothing goes wrong."

"What could go wrong?"

Clint shrugged. "Drunks, sore losers, maybe somebody trying to disrupt business."

"To what end?"

"Forcing her out of business."

"Now who'd want to do that?" Big Jack asked.

Clint leaned forward.

"Whoever would want to do it, I would advise against it," he said. "Anybody who wants to force Ashley out of business will have to go through me."

"You're new here, Adams," Big Jack said. "You're seeing threats where they don't exist. I'll be at the opening party tomorrow night to wish Miss Burgoyne only the best."

"I'll be there, too, Mackey," Clint said. "And I'll have my eye on you."

"That sounds like a threat, Mr. Adams," Big Jack said. "Please be aware that I have many contacts in Omaha."

"Good for you," Clint said. "The only contact I have is me—and I depend on me very heavily."

He stood up.

"I don't appreciate that you came into my place to threaten me, Adams. I'm not impressed with your reputation."

Clint looked over at the bar, where the bartender was

standing still, watching him, his hands beneath the level of the bar.

"You got a shotgun under that bar?" he asked.

"That's right."

"You want to pull it out?"

The man didn't answer.

"Dan? That your name?"

"That's me."

"You want to pull that shotgun, your boss dies first, then you."

Slowly, Dan put his hands on top of the bar.

"Smart man."

Clint looked at Big Jack. The man hadn't moved. From what Clint could see of his suit, there was no gun beneath it.

"I didn't come here to threaten you, Mackey," Clint said. "Just to fill you in on the facts."

"Well, you did that. You can leave now."

"See you tomorrow night," Clint said, and left.

"Mr. Mackey?" Dan said as Clint Adams left.

"You did the right thing, Dan," Mackey said. "He would've killed us both."

"Yessir."

Big Jack looked at Dan, tossed his cloth napkin on top of the remains of his second breakfast.

"But he won't get the chance again," he said. "I promise you that."

"Yessir."

"Is your brother still around?"

"He is, sir."

"Will he work for me?"

"If you pay him enough."

"How's he going to like the chance to go up against the Gunsmith?"

"He'll like it," Dan said, "but you'll still have to pay him."

"Oh, I'll pay him," Big Jack Mackey said. "I'll pay him just fine."

TWENTY-SEVEN

At four o'clock the Palace was open and serving drinks, so when each of the men came in, carrying a shotgun, Ed Wright told them, "Back room, boys."

In the back room, Clint waited with Ashley, who was ready to look the four new men over.

The first to arrive was Gabe Falkner.

"Gabe, this is Miss Burgoyne, the owner."

"Ma'am."

"Hello, Gabe."

"Can I see the shotgun?" Clint asked.

Falkner handed it over. It was an over-and-under with some age on it, but it had been cared for properly.

"Nice gun," Clint said, handing it back. "Have a seat."

The second man to arrive was Otto Gerald. He introduced Gerald to Ashley, who seemed a bit dubious about Clint's choice. But she was prepared to back his decision as long as she didn't violently disagree.

Otto's shotgun was a side-by-side Greener of which Clint approved.

Third into the room Ben Atchison.

"I know you," Ashley said.

"Yes, ma'am," Atchison said. "I been in your place a time or two."

"Pick up a shotgun off that table, Ben," Clint said. "We're waiting for the fourth man to arrive."

They didn't have long to wait. Mike Lukas walked in, seemed to know Atchison, but had to be introduced to Falkner and Otto. Then he introduced the gambler to Ashley, and saw that Ed was correct. She did like the look of Lukas.

"Well," she said then, "I'll leave you gentlemen in Clint's capable hands, and I'll see you later tonight. Oh, and also tomorrow night at the party. You're all invited."

After she left, Clint said to them, "You may all be invited, but the fact is you'll be working the party. You'll make sure that nobody gets out of hand."

"What do we do exactly?" Otto asked.

"You'll all be at the party, but other than that, you'll work in twos. I'll decide how to pair you up later. Oh, and the shotguns. They're for show mostly."

"How's that work?" Atchison asked.

"You let loose with a shotgun in a crowded saloon and a lot of innocent bystanders are going to get hurt. So if you have to shoot in a crowd, you use your handgun."

"Then what do we do with the shotguns?" Otto Gerald asked.

"I'll tell you when it's time to use the shotguns," Clint said. "Nobody uses one before I say. Got it?"

THE OMAHA PALACE

They all nodded, and Mike Lukas said, "We got it."

"Okay," Clint said, "now let's go over the placement . . ."

Half an hour later they all came out of the back room and bellied up to the bar, holding their shotguns.

"Ed, beers for our new employees," Clint said. "They get two a night. Keep track, and tell the other bartenders to keep track."

"Gotcha."

Wright set up beers for the four security men, and for Clint.

"Do we got to wear uniforms?" Atchison asked.

"No uniforms," Clint said. "Just stay clean. You hear me, Ben?"

"I took a bath!" Atchison said.

"I know, and we all appreciate it. But get yourself some clean clothes, too."

"New clothes? On five dollars a week?"

Clint grinned and said, "Cheap clean clothes." He addressed all four men. "Atchison and Otto, back here at six. Lukas and Falkner, be here at midnight."

"Got it," Falkner said.

"Right," Lukas said.

"Don't come in here before," Clint said, "and if you drink someplace else, don't come to work drunk. Understand?"

They all nodded.

"Okay," Clint said. "See you all later."

He drank down half his beer, then turned and walked back to Ashley's office.

"Hey, bartender," Mike Lukas called when Clint was gone.

"Yeah," Wright said.

"Anythin' goin' on between Adams and the boss?"
"Not that I know of."
"She got a man?"
"Nope," Ed Wright said, "nobody regular."
"Not you?"
"Me?" Wright asked. "She's the boss. That's all."
Lukas nodded and said, "Good to know."

TWENTY-EIGHT

Clint entered Ashley's office. She was seated behind the desk and looked up at him.

"What did you think?" he asked.

"They seem okay."

"I discussed the schedule with them," he said, sitting. "Oh, and they'll be at the party tomorrow night, but not as guests. I want them to work. I want them to be seen."

Ashley shrugged and said, "That's up to you. But put it in writing for me, will you? So that I know the schedule."

"Will do."

"And now you have to get out there and start setting up your table, don't you?"

"I do," Clint said, standing back up. "I've got two of those boys coming in at six, the other two at twelve."

"Fine."

Clint walked to the door. He considered telling Ashley

about young Pete Brennan, and about talking to Big Jack, but decided against it.

"See you later," he said, and walked out of the office.

Atchison and Gerald came back in at six o'clock. Clint showed them where to sit, at opposite ends of the room. He decided to have a carpenter come in and build two risers, so that when they sat, they'd be able to look out over the entire room.

"Look," he said to both of them, "somebody may come in looking for trouble with me. If that happens, I'll handle it. You handle anything else that happens. Otto, you'll take the lead. You move first, and Ben, you'll watch his back."

"Got it," Otto said, and Atchison nodded.

"Okay, take your places."

They went to their corners, and Clint went to his table.

The evening started . . .

Karen came down to work the floor a little after seven. The other girls did the same. There were three of them working. Otto and Ben Atchison both spoke to the girls. Clint assumed they were telling them who they were. After initially speaking to them, they had no contact. That was good. The men weren't distracted.

The first sign of trouble was when one of the former security men came in. It was Ed Wright who fired him, so he went right to the bar. Clint could tell from the way he moved that he was drunk.

Clint attracted Otto's attention and pointed to the bar. Otto nodded. This was his first chance to prove his worth

THE OMAHA PALACE

with his hands. He set the shotgun down against the wall by his chair and walked to the bar.

". . . tellin' you to get out, Sam," Wright was saying.

"I wanna know why I got fired, Ed," the man said. "I ain't leavin'—"

He went to draw his gun but Otto was there. He put his hand on Sam's hand so that he wasn't able to draw the weapon.

"Yeah, you are leavin'," he said into Sam's ear.

He turned the smaller man around and walked him roughly out the door. Once outside he pushed him into the street, but not hard enough to knock him down.

"Don't come back," Otto said. "I won't go so easy on you next time."

"Just wanna know why I got fired, is all," Sam complained drunkenly.

"You weren't good at your job," Otto said. "It's that simple."

"Yeah?"

"Yeah."

Sam shrugged.

"Thanks," he said. "That's all I wanted ta know." He turned and lurched drunkenly away.

Otto walked back in, nodded to Clint, and went back to his position.

Clint thought Otto passed his first test with flying colors . . .

Clint had another good night at faro. Nobody was able to beat him. Nobody challenged him. Even the losers just slunk away without a word.

Karen came over a time or two, pressed her hip to his shoulder, and asked if he wanted a drink. He declined each time.

He kept an eye on his game, and an eye on the two new security men. At midnight the next two came in, Falkner and Lukas. Otto and Atchison left immediately. If they were going to drink, they would do it someplace else.

After midnight the night went smoothly. Clint was counting up his winnings and closing down his table when the last customer left and Ed Wright locked the door.

"We done?" Lukas asked.

"You're done," Clint said. "You can both go and get some sleep."

"Thanks," Lukas said.

The door to Ashley's office opened and she came into the room. All four men looked over at her.

"Did we have a good night, gentlemen?" she asked.

"Pretty damn good, boss," Wright said.

"The boys were just leaving," Clint said. "They did good."

"Excellent," she said. "Good night, gentlemen. And thank you."

"Night, boss," Falkner said, heading for the door.

"Good night, ma'am," Mike Lukas said, giving her a bold once-over.

"Don't call me ma'am," she said to him, "and I'll call you . . . Mike. Okay?"

"Yes, ma—boss."

Wright unlocked the door, let them out, and locked it again.

"And you?" she asked, looking at Clint.

"I did well," he said.

"We did well, right?"

"Right," he said, handing over her take.

Ed Wright went into the kitchen, leaving them alone. Old Man Brennan was already gone.

"Ready for bed?" she asked Clint.

"Ready to get some sleep."

"That's what I meant," she said. "I'm gonna get some sleep myself. Night, Ed!"

"Good night, boss!" he called from the kitchen.

She smiled at Clint and went upstairs to her room. Wright came out of the kitchen.

"I told you."

"Told me what?"

"That she'd like that Lukas."

"Oh, yeah," Clint said. "Good night, Ed."

"Night, Clint."

Ed was wiping down his bar as Clint went up the stairs to his own room.

TWENTY-NINE

Ashley came down in time to have breakfast with Ed Wright and Clint.

"We're closed today," she told them. "All day. We're getting ready for the party."

"Yes, boss," Wright said.

"Get Leo in here. I want this place spotless by tonight."

"Right," Ed said.

She looked at Clint.

"Your men know what to do?"

"They do," Clint said, "but I'll tell them again to make sure."

"The mayor is going to be here," she said. "The chief of police. The head of the town council. The rest of the council."

"And Big Jack Mackey," Clint said.

"Right. I want them all to be impressed. I want this place to sparkle."

"Yes, boss," Ed Wright said.

"And Ed, make sure the girls sparkle, too."

"Right."

"And your men," she said to Clint. "Try to get them not to look like they just got off a horse."

"I'll clean them up."

She went back to her breakfast then. Today she ate it all.

During Big Jack's first breakfast the batwing doors opened and a man walked in.

"Chris," Big Jack said. Chris Nickerson was Dan's brother—younger, leaner, meaner, good with a gun. Very good with a gun.

"I hear you're lookin' for me."

"Have a seat, some coffee," said Big Jack.

"I'd rather have whiskey," Chris said, sitting.

"This early?"

"It's a wake-me-up."

Big Jack looked over at Dan. "Bring your brother some whiskey."

Dan came around, set a glass and a bottle in front of his brother.

"Thanks."

Chris poured himself a generous drink, downed it, and poured another.

"What's the job?"

"Dan didn't tell you?"

"No."

Big Jack looked over at the bartender, who was expressionless.

"Okay," he said. "Clint Adams. You know who he is?"

"The Gunsmith."

"Right. He's in town. He's gonna get in my way."

"Whataya want me to do?"

"I want you to get him out of my way."

"Today?"

"No," Big Jack said, "I don't want you to do anything until after tonight."

"Tonight's the party, right?"

"Right."

"Am I invited?"

"No."

Chris grinned, had another drink.

"Okay. What do I get paid?"

"Double."

"Triple," Chris said.

"Triple it is," Big Jack said. "Just be available, and don't do anything until I say so."

Chris held his glass up to Big Jack and said, "You're the boss."

After breakfast Ashley went back upstairs.

"I got to find Leo," Wright said.

"Have you seen him lately?"

"Not since you kicked him out of here yesterday."

"I didn't kick him out," Clint said. "I just didn't give him a job. He already has a job."

"And I got to make sure he does it."

"I have to do the same with my boys," Clint said. "So let's get started."

They left the saloon, and Ed Wright locked the doors behind them.

"See you back here in a couple of hours," Clint said. "I have to get myself some new clothes as well."

"Lucky I'm the bartender," Ed said. "I get to dress like one."

They split up from that point, Ed going off to find Leo, and Clint to find his four security men.

THIRTY

Clint found Falkner first. He was having breakfast in a café. While he wasn't sitting in the window, he was visible from it.

Clint entered, joined him at his table.

"You're up early for somebody who had the late shift," he said.

"I don't need that much sleep. Coffee?"

"Sure."

There was another cup on the table, upside down. Falkner righted it, and filled it.

"Thanks," Clint said.

"This a coincidence, or were you lookin' for me?" Falkner asked.

"I was looking for all of you, happened to see you in the window. Taking a chance, aren't you?"

"Beein' seen from the window?" Falkner asked. "I ain't no money gun, Clint. I'm not afraid to sit in the window. Not like you."

"I'm not afraid."

"No, but you know enough to be careful."

"It's how I've lived this long," Clint said.

"I get it."

"The others asleep?"

"I don't know," Falkner said. "We all work for you, but we ain't friends."

"You don't know anything about them?"

"Nope."

"Well, I need you all to be dressed decent tonight," Clint said.

"By decent, you mean clean."

"Right. If you see the others before I do, let them know, will you?"

"Sure. I can do that." He speared a big hunk of steak with his fork and stuck it in his mouth.

Clint drank the coffee, set the cup down, and stood up.

"Thanks for the coffee."

"Anytime."

"The party starts at seven," Clint said. "Be there at six, will you?"

"Sure."

"See you then."

"Shotguns tonight?"

"Shotguns every night," Clint said.

"You really expectin' trouble?"

"Oh yeah," Clint said, "I'm expecting trouble."

"Maybe we should have asked for more money," Falkner said.

Clint grinned and said, "I would have."

THIRTY-ONE

Mike Lukas had a room at the Omaha House Hotel. The knock at his door woke him. He stumbled to it, wearing only his underwear, and opened it.

"Oh, wait . . ." he said, and started to withdraw.

Ashley smiled and said, "Don't get dressed on my account."

"But—"

He backed away and she entered the room, closing the door behind her.

"How do you feel about forward women?" she asked.

"I guess that depends on how forward they are," he answered.

She smiled, reached out, and yanked his underwear down to his ankles. His penis sprang into view, and she looked properly impressed.

"Oh my," she said, taking it in one hand.

"Well," he said, looking down at himself in her hand, "I guess I don't mind it so much."

She got down on her knees, said, "Um," and took him in her mouth . . .

Clint found Otto and Atchison having breakfast together in another restaurant.

"Good mornin', boss," Atchison said. "Coffee?"

"I had enough," Clint said. "I just have a message for you two."

He told them what he'd told Falkner.

"We don't gotta buy expensive clothes, do we?" Atchison asked.

"No," Clint said, "I'm just reinforcing what I said yesterday. Cheap, but clean."

"We got it," Otto said.

"Either of you know where Lukas is staying?"

"Omaha House," Otto said.

"Either of you know anything about him?"

"Nope," Otto said.

"Nope," Atchison echoed.

"Okay," Clint said. "Be at the Palace at six. I'll see you both then."

"Right, boss," Otto said.

Clint left them to the rest of their breakfast.

Ashley sucked Lukas's cock until he thought his head was going to come off. Then she pushed him down on the bed, lifted her skirts, and mounted him.

"Don't you wanna get naked?" he asked.

"Shh," she said. "Later."

THE OMAHA PALACE 131

She didn't tell him that whether or not he got to see her naked depended on how well he fucked her. So far she was impressed with the way his cock had felt in her mouth, and the way he'd held up under her oral ministrations.

Now she wanted to see how long she could ride him before he exploded . . .

Clint walked up to the desk clerk at the Omaha House Hotel.

"What room is Mike Lukas in?"

"Mr. Lukas? Um . . ." The clerk looked nervous.

"Is he alone?"

"Um, no, sir."

"Okay," Clint said. "Just give me the room number. I won't interrupt him."

"Yessir," the clerk said. "Room seven."

"Thanks."

Clint went outside the hotel to wait.

Ashley rode Mike Lukas's cock for a long time, first slowly, then faster. Before long she was bouncing up and down on him, and the room was filled with the sound of their wet flesh slapping together.

He gritted his teeth and stayed with her the whole way. When she finally spasmed on top of him, he allowed himself to explode inside her. She gasped, cried out, and used her insides to milk him for all he was worth.

When she climbed off him, his cock flopped onto his belly.

"Jesus Christ," he gasped.

She stood, straightened her skirts, then looked at him.

"Are you gonna get undressed?" he asked her.

"Next time," she said.

"There's gonna be a next time?" he asked hopefully.

"Oh yes," she said, straightening her hair. "And in my room."

"Okay."

"Get some rest," she said. "You'll need to be sharp and awake tonight."

"In your room?" he asked with a grin.

"No," she said, "at my party. Be there at six."

"Yes, boss."

"Remember that."

She smiled at him and left the room.

Clint wasn't surprised when Ashley came down the stairs to the Omaha House lobby. He crossed the street and stayed out of her sight as she came out. She looked both ways, smoothed down her skirt, and then walked off.

Clint crossed the street, entered the hotel, and went upstairs to room seven.

When the knock came at his door, Mike Lukas couldn't believe it. Was she back for more already? He got up on rubbery legs, this time pausing to pull on his pants before answering the door.

"You look surprised," Clint said.

"I am," Lukas said. "Come on in, boss."

THIRTY-TWO

"Not a good idea," Clint said as he entered.

"What's that?" Lukas asked. He sat on the bed and vigorously rubbed his face.

"Sleeping with the boss."

Lukas looked at him.

"I saw her leave."

"That a problem for you?" Lukas asked. "I heard you and her weren't involved."

"We're not," Clint said.

"So then no problem."

"Not for me," Clint said, "but maybe for you."

"You gonna fire me?"

"Nope," Clint said, "just telling you to be careful. She tell you when to be at work tonight?"

"Yeah, six."

"And I don't have to tell you how to dress, right?" Clint said.

Lukas just gave him a look.

"Yeah, right," Clint said. "Get some rest, Mike. See you later."

Lukas just waved as Clint went out the door.

If Ashley liked being with Mike Lukas, there might be trouble coming from inside. Clint was sure the other girls were going to like him, too. And for a man like Lukas, working in the Palace might be like a kid in a candy store. But that wasn't his business. It wasn't up to him to watch for trouble within; it was his job to watch for it from without.

Clint went back to the Palace, recalling that Ed had locked the doors. If the bartender wasn't there, he would be locked out. Luckily, that was not the case. One of the double doors was unlocked, and as he entered, he saw Wright behind the bar.

"Hey, Ed. Get the job done?"

"Sure did. You?"

"Yup. How about a beer?"

"Comin' up."

Clint looked over at Leo, who was working on the floor with a mop. All the chairs were up on tables. That would be his next chore.

"I see you found Leo."

"I did. I had to drag him back here. Seems he's still a little miffed at you."

"How'd you get him back here?"

"I told him he'd be lettin' the boss lady down. He's still in love with her, so he came."

"Poor kid."

"Yeah, poor lovesick kid."

THE OMAHA PALACE

"You better keep an eye on him," Ed said. "Hickok had Jack McCall; you may have Leo."

"You think he hates me that much?"

"I think he does."

"And he's got the nerve to use a gun?"

"That I don't think he has."

"Even in the back?"

"Especially in the back. Just the same, though."

"Yeah," Clint said. "I'll keep an eye on him."

"I got some cases of champagne in the back I got to bring up here."

"I'll help you."

"That's okay. I'll get Leo—"

"No, let him finish what he's doing," Clint said. "I'll help you."

THIRTY-THREE

Clint came down from his room just before the party started. He was wearing a new suit he had bought that afternoon. In each corner of the room were Otto, Atchison, Falkner, and a weary-looking Mike Lukas. They all had their shotguns and their side arms.

Clint walked over to the bar, where Ed Wright was standing. The bartender was dressed in a white shirt, and his hair was parted down the center.

"Beer?" Ed asked.

"Sure."

As he poured, he said, "Doors open in ten minutes."

"I know. Is Ashley in her office?"

"Still upstairs."

"Think she'll be down?"

"Oh, she'll make an entrance," Ed said. "That'll leave you and me to entertain the guests until she does come down."

"Well," Clint said, "I guess we might as well go ahead

and open the doors early, then." He finished his beer and put the empty mug on the bar for Ed to whisk away, then went to the door.

The first group to arrive were the merchants and well-off townspeople who had been invited. After that the politicians began to arrive: the mayor, the head of the town council, and the chief of police.

"Mr. Adams," the chief said.

"Chief. Have some champagne."

"Don't mind if I do. Oh, this is our mayor, Warren Wilson."

Clint shook the big man's damp, soft hand and also invited him to the bar for champagne.

Finally, Big Jack Mackey arrived—alone. He walked in like he owned the place, and smiled expansively when he saw Clint.

"Fine place, Adams, fine place. And where is the lovely owner?"

"Oh, she'll be down directly. Why don't you go to the bar and have some champagne?"

"Don't mind if I do."

The place was starting to fill up, and when Clint looked up, he saw Ashley at the top of the stairs, looking out over the place. This was what she had been waiting for. He walked over so that he was waiting for her at the bottom when she got there.

"You look stunning," he said, and she did in a scoop-necked green gown that showed off a swollen cleavage.

"I can hardly breathe," she said, "but it's worth it."

She put her hand on his arm, and he escorted her around the room so she could greet her guests.

THE OMAHA PALACE

First the mayor, then the head of the town council, both men looking properly impressed by her gown. Then some of the merchants, and the town doctor.

Finally, they reached Big Jack, who was standing with a trio of town merchants.

"Ah, Miss Burgoyne," he said. "How beautiful you look tonight."

"Why, thank you, Mr. Mackey. How kind of you to say." She included the other men in her gaze as she asked, "Have you all had enough champagne?"

She waved over one of the girls, who were walking around the room with trays of champagne glasses. This one happened to be Karen, who came over and waited while the men replaced their empties. She met Clint's eyes only once, but then lowered her gaze.

"A toast, gentlemen!" Mackey said in a loud, blustery voice. "To the beautiful lady and her Palace! We wish her the best of luck!"

Clint marveled at how good a liar Big Jack Mackey was. Anybody watching him and listening to him would think he was telling the truth and he really wished Ashley well.

All the men in the room drank to the toast, and Clint noticed that the only women in the room were Ashley and the girls who worked for her. None of the men had bothered to bring their wives—or the wives had refused to come.

The party went on, with Ashley trying to pay attention to all of her important guests. At one point Clint noticed Big Jack standing on the side with the police chief. The younger Brennan was nowhere to be found. Clint wondered if the police chief knew that his young officer was also a confidant of Big Jack Mackey.

Clint grabbed a glass of champagne from a passing girl's tray—not Karen—and carried it over to where the two men were standing.

"Doing business at a party, gents?" he asked.

Both men looked at him with guilty expressions, as if they were caught doing something they shouldn't be doing.

"No business," Big Jack said. "We're just commenting on how lovely our hostess is."

"A lovely, lovely lady," the chief said.

"Well," Clint said, "you fellas have something in common."

"What's that?" the chief asked.

"You know a lovely woman when you see one."

"That doesn't take much," Big Jack said.

"You're right," Clint said. "You've got something else in common, too."

"What's that?" the chief asked.

"Secrets," Clint said. "You've both got secrets."

"Lots of people have secrets," Big Jack said.

"Yeah, but you two share them," Clint said. "You're both after the same thing. Only you"—Clint pointed at Big Jack—"you're in charge."

"Now see here—" the chief started.

"Why don't you go and get yourself some more champagne, Chief," Big Jack said.

"But he can't—"

"Go on," Mackey said more forcefully.

Clint could see the chief wanted to protest, but in the end he walked away.

"Does he know you're also using his man, Brennan?" Clint asked.

"No, he doesn't," Big Jack said. "But how do you know?"

"I keep my eyes open, Mackey," Clint said.

Big Jack looked around.

"I see you've got yourself some new security," he commented.

"I do," Clint said. "I'll bet I've got three men here I can trust."

"Three?"

"Well, yeah," Clint said. "I'm pretty sure one of them works for you."

The man just looked at him.

"I haven't figured out which one it is yet, but I will. Don't worry."

"I don't know what you're talking about, Adams," Big Jack said. "Excuse me."

The man walked off to join another group of men, who were deep in conversation.

Clint looked at each of his men in turn. Gerald, Atchison, Falkner, and Lukas. He was now certain that one of them worked for Big Jack. He was going to have to talk with Ed again the next day, go back and find out how each of the four men was sent to him, and how much the bartender really knew about each of them.

"Champagne, sir?"

He turned to see Karen holding a tray out to him.

"No, thanks."

"Oh, please, sir," she said. "The tray is so heavy."

He grinned and said, "All right, then," and took a glass.

"Ah, that's better," she said. "Thank you, sir."

She went off to distribute more of her burden.

THIRTY-FOUR

The party went on and Ashley continued to share the room. Clint continued to watch his four security men to see if any of them spoke with Big Jack, or even exchanged a glance.

He found himself at the bar with Ed Wright, decided to broach the subject right away rather than wait until the next day.

"Wait," Ed said. "Say that again?"

"I figure one of our four new security men works for Big Jack Mackey."

"What makes you say that?"

"I suspected it," Clint said, "so I braced him about it. His answer convinced me."

"Well, which man?"

"That's what I want you to help me figure out," Clint said. "How well do you know the four of them?"

"Pretty well," Ed said. "Look, Clint, if I didn't think we could trust them, I never would have sent them to you."

"I know that, Ed," Clint said. "But one of them is still on Big Jack's payroll. We've got to find out which one it is."

"Why don't you ask them?"

"Well, first, whoever it is will lie," Clint said. "I would. And second, I don't want the other three to think I suspect them."

"But you do."

"Yeah, but I don't want them to know," Clint said. "So we've got to figure this out ourselves."

"When?"

"Tomorrow," Clint said. "We'll get together and go over what you know about them."

"Okay."

One of the girls came over with a tray of empty glasses. She gave Clint a pretty smile while Ed removed the empties and replaced them with full glasses.

"Off you go, sweetie," Ed told her.

"Should I bring some to the guards?" she asked.

"No," Clint said, "they're not drinking."

"Okay."

She turned and walked away with a saucy swish to her butt.

"Now that one . . ." Ed said, watching her.

"I'll leave that to you, Ed," Clint said. "But let's talk at breakfast tomorrow morning."

"What if the boss is there?"

"She won't be," Clint said. "She won't rise early, not after tonight."

"Are we gonna let her know what we suspect?" the bartender asked.

"No," Clint said. "After we figure it out, we'll tell her what we know, not what we suspect."

"Okay."

Clint took a full glass of champagne from the bar and moved away.

Later, as the crowd began to thin out, Clint found himself standing next to the mayor.

"Mayor Wilson."

"Mr. Adams, isn't it?"

"That's right."

"So how long will the Gunsmith be in our fair city?" the man asked.

"I don't know," Clint said. "As long as I'm needed, I suppose."

"And how long might that be?"

"I guess that'll depend on your friend."

"My friend?"

"Big Jack."

"What does Mr. Mackey have to do with it?"

"I think you know, Mr. Mayor," Clint said. "I won't allow him to run Miss Burgoyne out of business."

"I don't know anything about such things, Mr. Adams," the mayor said.

"I'll stop him," Clint said, "and I'll take down anyone who's on his side. Understand?"

The mayor frowned and said, "I'm sure I don't—"

"Yeah," Clint said, "you understand. You tell him what I said."

"Mr. Mackey is an important man in this town," the mayor said, "and you are just passing through."

"That's what he keeps telling you, right? That he's important? And you believe it."

"I believe it's time for me to go."

"I think so, too, Mr. Mayor."

The mayor put down his unfinished drink and headed for the door. Along the way, Big Jack joined him then looked over his shoulder at Clint, who tossed him a salute.

THIRTY-FIVE

Outside, the mayor said to Big Jack, "That's a dangerous man."

"Don't worry, Mayor," Big Jack said. "I'll handle Clint Adams."

"You'd better," the mayor said. "After all, it looks like you're the reason he's in town, so you get him out of town"—he poked Mackey once in the chest—"before he does any damage. Irreparable damage."

"Don't worry, Warren," Big Jack said. "I'll handle it."

"Good night," the mayor said, and walked off to go home to his fat wife.

Big Jack thought the mayor was right. Adams was too dangerous to leave on his own. Tomorrow he and Chris were going to have to discuss different scenarios for getting rid of him.

He stepped off the boardwalk and headed home, where Janice was waiting.

* * *

Inside, Ed locked the doors and then returned to the bar.

"Good night, girls," Ashley said to her three saloon girls.

"Night, boss," one of them said, and all three went up to their rooms.

She walked to the bar, where Clint was drinking a beer to wash away the taste of all the champagne. At the other end of the bar the four security men were also having a beer each, to close out the night.

"Is she any good?" she asked.

"Who?"

"Karen," Ashley asked. "She is the one you're sleeping with, isn't she?"

"And how's Mike?" Clint asked.

"Oh, I think he'll do," she said, "for a while."

Clint wondered if she'd still think so if it turned out that Mike Lukas was the one working for Big Jack Mackey.

"You clean up, Ed," she said. "I'm going to bed. Good night, boys."

"Night, ma'am," Otto said, and the others echoed him.

They all watched her as she went up the stairs, and it was obvious—given the sway of her hips—that she knew they were watching.

"Finish up, boys," Ed called out. "Gotta start cleanin' up."

The four men downed their beers, then followed the bartender to the front doors.

"Night, Clint," Falkner called out.

Clint waved and the others waved back.

Ed Wright locked the doors behind them and returned to the bar.

"That was some party," he said.

THE OMAHA PALACE

"Really?" Clint asked. "I was expecting more."

"Like what?"

"I don't know . . . entertainment? Maybe somebody singing a song, doing some dancing? I don't know . . . something."

"We're not a dance hall, Clint," Ed said.

"That's true enough," Clint said.

"I saw you jawin' with Big Jack and with the mayor," Ed said. "What was that all about?"

"Just letting them know what's going on," Clint said. "I want them fighting among themselves."

"It ain't only the mayor that Big Jack's got in his pocket," Ed said. "You gotta think about the town council, and the police chief—"

"Not to mention Pete Brennan."

"What?" Ed asked. "The old man's boy?"

"Yep," Clint said. "I saw Police Officer Brennan in a restaurant with Big Jack."

"I wonder if Mike knows about that."

"I don't know," Clint said, "but I ain't about to ask him. If he does know, he'll tell his boy I asked. I don't want to let that little cat out of the bag yet."

"So we can't trust any of the four of 'em?"

"Nope," Clint said. "Not until we know."

"And we can't trust Mike, because of his son?"

"Right."

"So who can we trust?"

"Well, Ashley . . . and me."

Wright looked surprised.

"Not me?"

"For all I know, Ed, Big Jack put you in here before I got

here," Clint said. "And you helped him put one of the other men in. How'd you get this job?"

"I came in and interviewed for it."

"Out of the blue?"

"The blue? I heard she was looking for a bartender, and I came in."

"Where'd you work before?"

"A little saloon at the south end of town," he said.

"So you never worked for Big Jack?"

"No, never. Clint . . . you can trust me."

Clint stared at him a few seconds, then said, "Okay."

"Okay, you trust me?"

"Okay, I'll think about it," Clint said. "That's the best I can do, Ed."

"Yeah," Wright said, "yeah, okay. I gotta clean up a bit before I turn in. Then I'll finish up in the mornin'."

"Yeah, okay."

If Ed Wright was telling the truth, Clint would feel bad, but if Wright was working for Big Jack, then Clint couldn't trust him.

He went up to the second floor and knocked on Ashley's door. She answered wearing a dressing gown, with a brush in her hand.

"I wake you up?"

"I was just brushing my hair," she said. "Is this business? Or can it wait?"

"Business."

"Come on in."

He entered and she closed the door behind them.

"What's this about?"

THE OMAHA PALACE

"Ed."

"My bartender? What about him?"

"Can you trust him?"

She hesitated, then said, "Well, I thought I could. Until you just asked me. What's on your mind?"

"I'm thinking Big Jack put a man in here, maybe one of the four new ones. But what if he put Ed in here first?"

"And Ed recommended the four men," she said. "So one, two, three, or all of them could be working for Big Jack also."

Clint shrugged.

"I don't think all," he said. "I think one. And I might be wrong, but . . . I just started thinking about Ed, too."

She sat in front of her mirror and started brushing her hair.

"Clint, can we afford to distrust everyone?" she asked. "What about the girls?"

"I know, I know," Clint said. "You're probably right. I'm being too distrustful. We should go back to thinking that maybe Big Jack has put one man inside."

She turned to face him.

"I think so."

"All right," he said. "I'm sorry I bothered you with this. I did talk with both Big Jack and the mayor tonight. He's got the mayor, the chief of police, and a few other influential men in his pocket."

"I figured that when I first came here and made plans to open the Palace. But I went ahead anyway. Maybe I was wrong, but I'm committed now."

"We're committed now," he said. "I'll stay on as long as you need me."

"Even if you have to go up against every influential man in town?"

"I think they should have to worry about going up against me," he said. "You get some rest. I'll see you in the morning."

"Good night, Clint."

He left her room and walked down the hall to his own. He wondered how she intended to get Mike Lukas up to her room. Back door left open?

He opened his own door, found Karen sitting on his bed, waiting.

THIRTY-SIX

Clint woke in the morning with Karen's head on his belly. She was asleep, her breath gentle and warm on his skin. Once again, she had tired him out during the night, yet he was awake and she was asleep.

He tried to slip out from beneath her. She was sleeping so soundly that he was able to do it. He also moved about the room washing and dressing, without her stirring,

He slipped out of the room and down the stairs. When he got there, Ed was drinking coffee. The place had been cleaned up, and Leo was taking chairs off tables.

"Morning," Ed said.

"Good morning."

"Mike's makin' breakfast."

"Good."

Clint sat down. There was a chill coming from Ed's side of the table.

"Look," Clint said. "about last night—"

"Don't worry about it," Ed said. "Let's just do what we gotta do. You'll find out eventually that you can trust me."

"Okay," Clint said.

Mike Brennan appeared then with their breakfast.

"Don't bring a plate for Miss Burgoyne, Mike," Clint said. "She'll be down later."

"I know," Brennan said, and left.

"He has an instinct for when she'll come down early and when she won't," Ed said.

"I didn't mean to insult him."

"Like you noticed," Ed said, "Mike's in a mood. I ain't figured it out yet. He's usually kinda testy, but lately he's been worse."

"Maybe it's his son."

"But he's a policeman."

"The job may not appeal to Mike," Clint said.

"Well, let's eat before it gets cold."

They both started.

"Tell me about the four men," Clint said.

"What do you want to know?"

"How do you know them?"

"In passing mostly," Ed said. "I've known Otto the longest. He works jobs all over town, and for a while we worked in the same saloon. If you trusted me, you'd know you can trust him, because I do."

"I felt that about Otto when I met him," Clint said. "I don't think he works for Big Jack."

"So okay," Ed said.

"What about Atchison?"

"He's been in here to drink a few times since we opened," Ed said. "Sometimes when nobody else is around, so we've talked."

"What's he doing in Omaha?"

"He heard the town was growing, becoming a city," Ed said. "He thought this might be the place for him to settle down. Only he ain't been able to find a job."

"Until now."

"Well, when you said you was lookin' for men, I just thought . . . why not?"

"Trust him like you trust Otto?"

Ed paused, then said, "No."

"Okay, how about Falkner?"

Ed hesitated, then said, "I gotta tell you the truth. I knew Falkner in Abilene, saw him kill a man there. He's good with a gun, and I thought that was what we needed."

"What's he doing in Omaha?"

"Passin' through," Ed said. "Not lookin' for a place to settle."

"And he hires his gun out?"

"Naw, he ain't a money gun, if that's what you're thinkin'," Ed said. "But he knows how to handle one. I thought he'd be the best for what you wanted."

"And Lukas?"

"A gambler," Ed said. "Came to town, hit a bad streak. He was just lookin' for a stake."

"Five dollars a week?"

"Hey," Ed said, "he took it."

"But why?"

"Maybe you should ask him," Ed said. "To tell you the truth, he's the one I know the least. I was talkin' to somebody else about the job, and Lukas was nearby. He heard me, said he'd take the job."

"So when I asked you if anybody approached you . . ." Clint said.

"Right," Ed said. "I shoulda said he did, but I didn't think of it that way."

"Well," Clint said. "I guess I should start with him."

"Do you know where he is?" Ed asked. "Where he's stayin'?"

Clint looked up. "I don't know where he's staying, but I might know where he is."

THIRTY-SEVEN

Clint was standing in the back of the building, leaning against the wall, when the back door opened and Mike Lukas stepped out. His shirt had not yet been buttoned up.

"Mornin'," Clint said.

"Uh-oh," Lukas said. "Jealous boyfriend? I thought you said—"

"Not jealous," Clint said. "Curious. Can I buy you some coffee?"

"Make it breakfast and okay."

"Let's go," Clint said, "but you better button up."

Clint led the way out of the alley.

Omaha seemed to be filled with small cafés. They found one and got seated. Clint never thought he could get his fill of coffee, but it was happening.

"Breakfast?" the waiter asked.

"Just coffee for me."

"Ham and eggs, and coffee," Lukas said.

As the waiter left, Lukas looked at Clint and asked, "What's on your mind?"

"You are," Clint said. "I'm wondering why a gambler would take a five-dollar-a-week job."

"I need the money."

"Five dollars. You can probably make more than that being a store clerk."

"I'd shoot myself in the head before I'd take a job in a store," Lukas said. "Or before I'd swamp out a barn. This job, at least, involves a gun, so I took it."

Clint frowned, sat back as the waiter came with coffee and poured it out.

"So what's this about?" Lukas asked.

Clint studied the man. Was he the one?

"I just want to make sure I can trust the four men I hired for security," he said.

"You think somebody's gonna try to steal from Ashley?" Lukas asked.

That was as good an excuse as any.

"I just don't want to see that happen," he said.

"Well, you can count on me," Lukas said. "I want to see Ashley succeed."

"So do I."

Clint sat with Lukas while the man ate his breakfast, and then the gambler went back to the rooming house he was staying in.

"See you this afternoon," he told Clint. "I've got the six o'clock shift."

"See you then."

THE OMAHA PALACE

Clint headed back to the Palace, but along the way he passed the sheriff's office, so he deiced to go in.

Sheriff Thorpe looked up from his desk as Clint entered.

"Adams."

"Sheriff," Clint said. "Thought I'd see you at the party last night."

"Really? I wasn't even invited."

"Mind if I sit?"

"Why not?" Thorpe said. "Coffee's on the stove."

"No thanks," Clint said. "I've had enough."

"Whiskey?"

"Too early."

"Not for me."

He took a bottle out of his desk and poured a couple of fingers into a mug. He replaced the bottle, then took a sip.

"What's on your mind?"

"I figure you know everybody in town."

"If I did, that would mean I was good at my job."

"I suspect you are."

"Was," Thorpe said, staring into his mug thoughtfully. "Maybe I was."

"Maybe you still are," Clint said. "Let's test it out."

Thorpe sat back in his chair, cradling his mug, and said, "What do you want?"

"I figure Big Jack Mackey's got the new law in his pocket," Clint said. "The chief, and even more."

"So?"

"Also the mayor, and the town council."

"You askin' me if he's got me in his pocket?"

"No," Clint said. "I don't think he does. But I'm wondering about some other men."

"Who?"

"We've hired four new men as security at the Palace," Clint said. "I want to know if I made a mistake."

"Hirin' the wrong men?"

Clint nodded.

"You think Mackey put one in there?"

"One or more."

"What do you want from me?"

"I want to tell you their names and hear what you have to say about each of them."

Thorpe sipped his whiskey, then put the mug down on his desk and said, "Okay, go ahead."

THIRTY-EIGHT

Big Jack Mackey woke up and slid out of bed without waking Janice. He'd fucked her silly the night before, so she didn't stir. He wondered how much longer he should keep her around, or should he go ahead and replace her? He probably should wait until he resolved the whole Palace issue.

He pulled on a silk robe, belted it, and went downstairs. The smell of breakfast wafted out from the kitchen. His cook, Mrs. Willis, usually came in early to prepare it.

He entered the kitchen. The heavyset, middle-aged woman turned and looked at him.

"Mornin'," she said.

She was usually cheerful, except when she knew that Janice was up in his bed.

"Good morning, Berta."

"Breakfast will be ready in ten minutes," she said. "For two?"

"Yes, please. In the dining room."

"Yes, sir."

She handed him a cup of coffee and he carried it into the living room with him. There was a knock at his door then, and he went to answer it.

"Mornin'," Chris Nickerson said.

"Come on, in," Big Jack said. "Breakfast is almost ready."

Mrs. Willis would be surprised when she came out of the kitchen and realized the second for breakfast was a man.

Clint listened carefully to Thorpe's opinions on the four men.

Otto Gerald: "As honest as they come. Hard worker."

Ben Atchison: "He won't last. He'll drift away eventually, but I don't think he's dishonest."

Gabe Falkner: "If I was still the only law in town, I'd pin a badge on him."

"He's that good?" Clint asked.

"Better."

"I'll keep that in mind."

Mike Lukas: "He's a gambler. I don't like him."

Clint wished the lawman had had another reason to dislike Lukas. Lots of his friends were gamblers, and in fact, he considered himself one.

He stood up.

"I appreciate your time, Sheriff."

Sheriff Thorpe sat forward, grabbed his mug from his desk.

"You think I helped?"

"Well," Clint said, "you've given me something to think about."

Clint headed for the door.

THE OMAHA PALACE

"Keep a close eye on Mackey," Thorpe said.

"I intend to."

"He's got plenty of resources you still don't know anythin' about."

Clint had his hand on the doorknob, paused to look at Thorpe.

"Anything or anyone in particular?"

Thorpe thought a minute, sipped his drink.

"Mackey's got a bartender named Dan," he said.

"I met him," Clint said. "Big, burly guy. You think I have to worry about him?"

"Not him," Clint said. "His last name's Nickerson."

Clint frowned.

"That name sounds familiar."

"Been gettin' around of late," Thorpe said. "His brother's name is Chris."

"Chris Nickerson," Clint said. "That's right. Supposed to be pretty good with a gun. Is he in town?"

"He could be," the lawman said. "I don't know for sure."

"He's supposed to have some boys riding with him."

"That's what I heard."

"I'm not going to be able to count on the police in this town," Clint said.

"That's for sure."

"How about you, Sheriff?" Clint asked. "Can I count on you, if it comes right down to it?"

"I'll do my job," Thorpe said, "if I'm allowed to."

"What's that mean?"

"I hear the town council's about to meet," he said. "My badge may be on the agenda."

"I see."

"Check back with me," Thorpe said. "If I'm still wearin' tin, you can count on me."

"And if you're not?"

Thorpe poured himself some more whiskey.

"Then maybe you'll need another security man at the Palace?"

THIRTY-NINE

Berta was much more cheerful when she brought out the breakfast for two and saw Chris Nickerson. She'd prepared a ton of eggs, bacon, and flapjacks, then served them with a basket of hot biscuits and some honey.

"This is the way to live," Nickerson said.

"That's why I'll crush anyone who tries to ruin it for me," Big Jack said.

"That what you think that woman is doin' with her saloon?" Nickerson asked, his mouth full of eggs.

"I do."

"Then you want me to take care of her?"

"In time," Big Jack said, "but first you'll have to handle the Gunsmith."

"I can do that."

"Not alone, though," Mackey said. "I don't want you to take any chances."

"I've got some good boys with me," Nickerson said. "You won't have to worry."

"Then eat hearty, Chris," Big Jack said. "I hope you don't mind killin' on a full stomach."

Nickerson stuck a large forkful of flapjacks into his mouth and said, "Never have before."

Clint went back to the saloon, back to his room. Karen was gone. So was her warmth from the sheets. He walked to the window and looked down at the street in front of the Palace. After he'd braced both the mayor and Big Jack at the party last night, and after talking with the sheriff, he was fairly sure they'd come for him—if not that day, then the next.

He didn't know how many would come. It would have been helpful to have somebody back his play, but he didn't know of anyone he could trust. According to the sheriff, Falkner was good with a gun. He could ask him. And then there was the sheriff. He didn't have any idea how good he'd be, or even if he'd be sober when the time came. But those were probably the only two men who had anywhere near the experience he needed.

Falkner had told him he was staying in a hotel in the south end of town. Clint left the room, went down to the saloon. Ed was behind the bar.

"How many hotels are there in the south part of town?" he asked.

"A couple. Fleabags, though. Why?"

"Falkner said that's where he was staying. I want to go talk to him."

"Want me to come with you?"

"No," Clint said, "you better stay here."

THE OMAHA PALACE

Ed frowned at him.

"You think somethin's gonna happen today?" he asked.

"It might."

"Maybe I better send for Otto, Atchison, and the others."

"Maybe you should," Clint said. "I'll get Falkner myself."

"Watch your back," Ed said. "It ain't so nice there as it is here."

"Is that beyond the deadline?"

"It sure is. Whores and opium dens and the works. All there."

"In Omaha?"

"When a town grows," Ed said, "the good comes with the bad, don't it?"

"I guess it does," Clint agreed.

Chris Nickerson stopped in at Big Jack's to talk to his brother.

"I'm goin' outside of town to get my boys," he said.

"Yeah?"

"The boss wants me to take care of Adams."

"So do it."

"You wanna come?"

"I ain't no gunman, Chris," Dan said. "I'm just a bartender. I belong back here, behind the bar."

"You're my brother, Dan," Chris said. "You belong with me."

"I'd getcha killed, little brother," Dan said. "If any trouble breaks out in here, I'm your man. But you're gonna be in the street. I ain't no good out there."

"I'll watch out for you."

"No," Dan said. "You go and do your job. I'll be waitin' for ya here."

"Dan—"

"You go on now," Dan said. "And don't take no chances with that man. Not that one."

FORTY

Ed was right.

Clint walked past whores' cribs, closed during the day, and opium dens, open all the time. One girl came out, wearing nothing but a wrap, and smiled at him with blackened teeth.

"No thanks," he said.

An older Chinese woman waved at him from a doorway, motioning for him to come into one of the dens.

"No thanks," he said again.

He got past them and started passing some falling-down buildings, some of which were residences, some saloons. Farther on, the buildings became sturdier. There were some proper saloons and cafés, and then two hotels.

He found Falkner registered in one of them, but the clerk said he wasn't there.

"Where is he?" Clint asked. "Do you know?"

"Try the dens."

"The dens? Not the cribs?"

"He won't touch no dirty whores," the man said. "The dens."

He retraced his steps, although he didn't know why. If Falkner was on the pipe, he wouldn't be much good. Might even have to fire him.

He tried two or three of the dens before he found the right one.

"I'm looking for a man called Falkner," he said to the Chinese woman—the same one who had beckoned to him before. Now she did so again, and he followed.

Inside were stacked bunks with nothing more than straw mattresses on them. This early many of them were empty, but some of them were occupied with men whose eyes were either closed, or bleary from the pipe.

Inside she held a pipe out to him, but he said, "No, I'm looking for a man."

She waved at him to go and look.

He found Falkner sitting on a lower bunk, pulling on his boots.

"Clint," the man said. "What are you doing here?"

"Well, I was looking for you," Clint said. "When they told me you were here, I thought . . ."

"You thought you'd find me deep in the pipe," Falkner said. "No. The opium is not for me."

"Then why do you come here?"

"To sleep," he said.

"You have a room for that."

"Sometimes it gets too noisy," he said. "Here it's quiet."

Clint inhaled the smell of stale opium smoke.

THE OMAHA PALACE

"But the smoke . . ."

"Oh, it gets kinda thick in here sometimes," Falkner said. "Maybe that's what helps me sleep."

"Why don't you just tell the hotel about the noise?" Clint asked. "Get it stopped."

Falkner stood up, strapped on his gun.

"The noise ain't in the hotel," he said. "It's in my head."

"Oh," Clint said.

"You've heard that noise yourself, I'm sure," Falkner said.

"I have, yeah," Clint said, understanding.

"What's on your mind?" Falkner asked. "Why were you lookin' for me?"

"You want some breakfast?" Clint asked, wondering if he could drink any more coffee. "We can talk."

"You buyin'?"

"I am."

"Good," Falkner said. "Wouldn't want to have to spend any of my five dollars a week."

FORTY-ONE

"What about the others?" Falkner asked half an hour later.

He had taken Clint to one decent café in that end of town. They served breakfast, but they also had beer, so Clint had that instead of more coffee. Falkner had bacon and eggs. And beer.

"I figure they should stay inside, in case Big Jack tries anything there."

"So just you and me?"

Clint nodded.

"Against how many?"

"I'm not sure how many men Nickerson's got."

"I heard as many as a dozen, as few as five. Nobody knows."

"Five would be all right."

"A dozen's too many, even for you."

"Probably. What about the sheriff?"

"He'd be okay, if he's sober," Falkner said.

"If he's even still sheriff."

"Might be better if he wasn't," Falkner said.

"Listen," Clint said, "I can't pay you to do this, well, I mean, I could, but—"

"I don't hire out my gun," Falkner said.

"That's what I heard."

"But I do loan it out sometimes."

They walked back to the saloon together, watching each other's backs on the busy Omaha streets.

"This crowd, it'd be perfect to try something now," Falkner said.

"Nickerson probably has to round up his men."

"You really think they'll try something today?"

"I pushed last night," Clint said. "I think Big Jack's the type to push right back."

"And all because of a new saloon?"

"Big Jack's got his hooks into this town pretty deep," Clint said. "He can't afford anyone cutting into his territory."

"And he thinks that's what Ashley's trying to do?" Falkner said. "And to do that, he's got to get rid of you first."

"That's what I'm thinking."

They stopped right in front of the Palace.

"Why not just burn it down?" Falkner asked.

"He might," Clint said, "but if he did it now, he knows I'd come after him."

"So you need him to send someone after you."

"And we need that someone to testify that he did."

"If you can keep him alive," Falkner said. "If Nickerson

THE OMAHA PALACE

comes after you with his men, he's the only one who'll know who's payin' the freight. That means you want to stop him without killin' him. I can't guarantee that."

"Well, if he ends up dead," Clint said, "we'll think of something else."

"Like putting a bullet in Big Jack?"

Clint looked at him.

"I'm not a murderer, Falkner."

"I'm not either," Falkner said. "Too bad. It'd be so easy."

They went inside.

Inside, Ed was standing at the bar with Gerald, Atchison, and Lukas. They all had a beer.

"What's goin' on?' Lukas asked. "Ed woke me up to come here early."

"Didn't have time to make any other stops?" Clint asked him.

"What other stops?"

"Maybe to let Jack Mackey know what's going on?"

Lukas had been leaning on the bar. Now he straightened up.

"What's that mean?"

At that moment Ashley came down the stairs, wearing a simple dress she must have put on quickly. She was patting her hair into place.

"What's going on?" she asked. "Why aren't we open?"

"I was waiting for Clint to let me know if we should," Ed said.

"Clint decides when we open now?"

"I do today," he said. "Let's go into your office and talk."

He took her arm to lead her back there, turned around, and said to Ed, "Don't open."

"Yessir."

"So what are you going to do?" Ashley asked. "Keep us closed up until they try something?"

"No," Clint said. "If I'm right, the mayor and the police chief will put pressure on Big Jack to do something quickly."

"Like today?"

"I hope so."

"So what next?"

"Keep the doors locked," Clint said. "I'm going to sit outside, in plain sight."

"Alone?"

"Falkner's going to watch my back."

"And the other three?"

"They'll stay inside and look after you, and the place."

"The place?"

"Well, like Falkner said," he replied, "it would be easier just to burn it down."

"Burn it down?" she said, aghast. "My place?"

"Let's hope not," Clint said. "Let's hope they come for me first, and Falkner and I can take care of them."

"You keep saying 'them,'" she said. "Isn't it Jack Mackey?"

"It's whoever Mackey pays to come after me."

"And do you know who that will be?"

"I have a good idea."

FORTY-TWO

Clint took a wooden chair outside with him, set it against the front of the building, and sat in it. Falkner was . . . somewhere. He didn't know exactly where.

He considered going to Big Jack's to talk to the bartender, maybe get him to take a message to his brother. But in the end he decided just to sit there . . . all day if he had to.

At midday Sheriff Thorpe came over, put one foot up on the boardwalk.

"Town council meet yet?" Clint asked.

"Oh, yeah," Thorpe said. "I'm supposed to turn my badge over tomorrow."

"So what are you doing today?"

"Well, so far I had a talk with Dan Nickerson."

"What'd he have to say?"

"His brother's got eight men with him. They'll be coming in today, before dark."

"And?"

"They'll pick a fight with you."

"And what will the police do?"

"Look the other way, I suppose."

"And you?"

"Me? I'm nobody tomorrow."

"But today you're still the law."

"Good point."

The sheriff walked across the street to the hardware store, went inside, came out with a chair, and sat down, almost directly across from Clint.

Three against eight, Clint thought. He could pull the others out of the saloon, but that might end badly, especially if Big Jack had somebody trying to get in the back to burn the place down.

He decided to stand pat with the hand he had.

Three aces, hopefully.

Chris Nickerson led his men to the edge of town. He stopped, turned in the saddle.

"Everybody know what to do?"

"Yeah," his number two, Tom Decker, said. "Kill the Gunsmith."

"And then we all get paid," someone else said, and the other men cheered.

Nickerson had never seen so many men in a hurry to kill.

"Are you sure we don't have to worry about the police?" another man asked.

"They won't be around."

THE OMAHA PALACE

"And the sheriff?" Decker asked.

"Drunk. That enough?"

They all nodded.

"Then let's go."

Officer Pete Brennan stopped in the chief's office.

"The men haven't gone out yet for the next shift," he said.

"I've asked them to be held back."

"Why?"

"Where does it say in your job description that I have to answer to you, Officer?" the chief asked. "The men will go out when I say so. And that includes you."

Brennan left the chief's office, changed out of his uniform, and left the building.

When Nickerson and his men came within view of the Palace, they saw Adams sitting out front.

The people on the street knew trouble when they saw it. The street was suddenly empty, but for the eight of them.

"Why's he waitin' there?" Decker asked.

"Because he believes his own reputation," Nickerson said. "Come on."

"We gonna ride right up to him?" Decker asked.

"Right up to him," Nickerson said, "and then we cut him down."

"You don't want a chance at him yourself first?" Decker asked.

Nickerson looked at him.

"That's not the job, Tom."

He started his horse forward, and the others followed.

* * *

The sheriff saw the eight men riding down the street toward Clint. He dropped the front legs of his chair down to the walk.

He was stone-cold sober.

Clint saw the riders, saw the sheriff drop his chair legs down, and hoped that wherever Falkner was, he could see them, too.

He didn't stand up.

Ashley looked out the window, saw the riders coming down the street. She turned and ran from the room.

FORTY-THREE

Nickerson reached Clint first. The others came after and fanned out. Clint was taken by surprise. He thought Nickerson would speak to him. They always talked first, men like that. Blustered. But this one was different. This man drew his gun, and the others followed.

Clint had no choice. As they started to fire, he stood up and leaped through the front window, broken shards of glass showering down . . .

The sheriff drew his gun and ran into the street. Two of the mounted men saw him, were surprised, but turned their guns on him.

Falkner came out of the alley he'd been hidden in, gun drawn, cursing himself for standing too far away. He saw Clint go through the window with a hail of bullets following him.

* * *

Ashley came running down the stairs, shouting at Ed and the others, "Clint's in troub—" but suddenly the front window exploded in. All the men turned, drawing their guns.

Clint hit the floor, turned, drew his gun, and began firing outside. Before he knew it, the others were beside him, shotguns firing.

Thorpe fired as he ran, took two men from their saddles. A bullet hit him in the thigh and he went down.

Falkner fired as he ran, saw a man fall from his saddle. Then he felt something strike his shoulder and he was on the ground.

Clint watched with little satisfaction as all the men were flung from their saddles, some from his bullets, some from the shotgun blasts. And suddenly it was quiet.

He climbed out the window, followed by the others.

"Check them," he called as he ran to where Thorpe had fallen.

When he reached the lawman Thorpe said, "I'm all right. Got me in the leg. Check on your friend."

Clint turned, saw Falkner on the ground. He ran over to him, turned him over, saw the wound in his shoulder.

"Damn it," Falkner said. "Must've been those damn opium fumes. I misjudged the distance."

"You'll be all right," Clint said. "Come on, I'll help you up."

He got Falkner to his feet as Ed Wright reached him.

"They're all dead," Ed said, "except the leader."

"Nickerson?" Clint said. "Well, that's handy."

FORTY-FOUR

Clint woke up the third morning after the shooting, rolled over, and pressed himself against Karen. His hard cock rested in the crack between her buttocks.

"Good morning," she said. "Still leavin' today?"

"Yes," he said with his mouth against her neck.

She shifted her legs so he could slide up between them and said, "Well, we better have a proper good-bye, then."

He went downstairs, found Ed and Ashley having breakfast. As he sat down, Mike Brennan came out and put a plate in front of him. He did it without a scowl.

"He's in a better mood," Clint said.

"Well, young Brennan did some running to help," Ed said. "Not his fault he got there too late to do anything but watch."

"Apparently," Ashley said, "father and son have made up."

"He did go with the sheriff and back his play when he arrested Big Jack," Clint said. "His final act as sheriff."

"Until the council rehired him the next day," Ed said.

"The chief couldn't let Mackey go?" she asked.

"Not without looking bad," Clint said. "After all, Nickerson talked."

"So now they're both in jail," Ed said.

"You think they'll stay there?" Ashley asked.

"Who knows?" Clint asked. "Mackey's still got a lot of money. He might be able to buy his way out of prison, but the people in this town won't want him around anymore."

"So you're leaving," she said.

"Yes. Right after breakfast."

"The others are staying, you know," she said. "I mean Otto, Ben, even Mike, even though you suspected him."

"I apologized for that," Clint said. "Looks like Big Jack didn't have an inside man."

"Or," Ed said, "if he did, he changed his mind."

Clint stared across the table at Ed Wright, who was suddenly concentrating on his breakfast.

Watch for

THE UNIVERSITY SHOWDOWN

368th novel in the exciting GUNSMITH series from Jove

Coming in August!

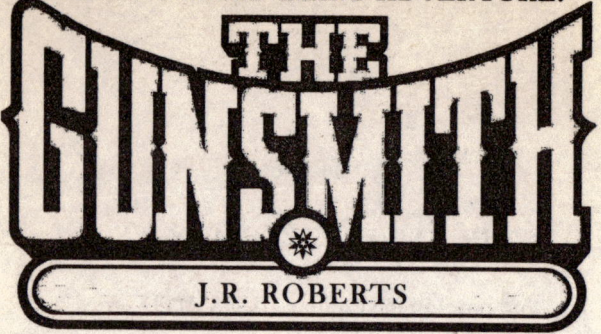

GIANT ACTION! GIANT ADVENTURE!

THE Gunsmith

J.R. ROBERTS

Little Sureshot And
The Wild West Show
(Gunsmith Giant #9)

Dead Weight
(Gunsmith Giant #10)

Red Mountain
(Gunsmith Giant #11)

The Knights of Misery
(Gunsmith Giant #12)

The Marshal from Paris
(Gunsmith Giant #13)

Lincoln's Revenge
(Gunsmith Giant #14)

Andersonville Vengeance
(Gunsmith Giant #15)

penguin.com/actionwesterns

M455AS0510

GIANT-SIZED ADVENTURE FROM AVENGING ANGEL LONGARM.

BY TABOR EVANS

2006 Giant Edition:

LONGARM AND THE OUTLAW EMPRESS

2007 Giant Edition:

LONGARM AND THE GOLDEN EAGLE SHOOT-OUT

2008 Giant Edition:

LONGARM AND THE VALLEY OF SKULLS

2009 Giant Edition:

LONGARM AND THE LONE STAR TRACKDOWN

2010 Giant Edition:

LONGARM AND THE RAILROAD WAR

penguin.com/actionwesterns

Jove Westerns put the "wild" back into the Wild West

SLOCUM by
JAKE LOGAN

Don't miss these exciting, all-action series!
penguin.com/actionwesterns